The Cries of the Pews

Beyond The Pulpit

S.A. Wilkinson

This book is dedicated to my Grandmother Edna White "Memaw", who taught me that no matter who you are or where you come from your worth is the same as anyone else. She showed me that everyone deserves a chance for their story to be told and never to judge people according to their outside because there's always another picture inside that you can't see. I learned a lot growing up on Sunset Avenue and I miss my Memaw dearly.

I also dedicate this book to my parents Paul and Helen Andry who always let me push. Even when I was a child, they never set boundaries or limits concerning me. I always had the entire field to run but I had to run my fastest. It taught me that in life, there are never any limits or restrictions just high expectations. You have to give it your all! It made me who I am today. Thanks momma. Thanks daddy!

I'd also like to thank Sherry Reynolds, Brandon Johnson, Doreen Harbison, Kimberly Bradley, Leonard Perryman, Kristina Davis and Francine Pina-Council for helping me make this happen. Dr. Joseph L. Williams and Rosalind Bishop thank you for encouraging me every step of the way!

Thanksgiving of 2013, I shared this book with my family. This book is a "God thing" for me. One of those ideas that you know you would have never had on your own but could have only come from God. That's exactly what this was - from the title, to the images, even down to all of its content. I can't explain it, other than; it was a "must do" assignment. God said, "DO IT" and don't ask any questions. The time-lapse between when the assignment was given and its completion, is an entirely different story. Nonetheless, we're here.

Anyone that knows me, know, that justice is closer to my heart than anything! My husband, Don, refers to me as "The Fixer." I am always looking for "the solution". I believe if you have a story, you should tell it. If you can't tell it for whatever reason, you should have someone else to do it! So here I go, I am doing it...finally. Many people will spend their time "trying to figure out" the characters of this book and that's okay BUT, that's not the point. A lot of people will read these stories and think of themselves or a loved one or take these confessions and use them as a mirror to their inner thoughts and soul.

In either instance, justice has been served because a release from hurt or pain has occurred by simply telling the story. Healing, which is long overdue, has arrived on these pages. It's now my prayer that victory begins!

-Steph

CONTENTS

Introduction

There are many cries that come from the pews on Sunday mornings. Some last for seconds, minutes or even hours after the service has ended. Some have lasted a lifetime. The tears that flow are those of joy, deliverance and pain, caused by the very place where they were birthed. These tears are filled with the salt of heartache and for some, the silent sound of surrender. Years of pain sit in these pews. Decades of despair lay behind these doors.

Why are their voices and cries ignored? Why is the hurt permitted? Why is the victim the least to be forgiven? The biggest question is why does it continue to go on? It's as if a wrong has been baptized and made right. It's now a law that has no validation but yet upheld. It is a lower standard with a higher accountability. It's Sunday morning and here it all begins. These are their true confessions, their broken hearts, the endless nightmares and their lonely tears.

People say it all the time. Sunday mornings are the most segregated time of the week. It's the time no matter your race or denomination that you and your world worship. The one common denominator is that every church and chapel is filled with people. The pews are filled with all walks of life. They all have a heart, a voice and more importantly, a story. Some are the tales of victory and overcoming. Others have voices that are filled with anguish and hurt.

No matter the origin, a cry is still a cry. The release that is felt when the story is told is like the release of poison from a snake bite that is trapped under the skin of a victim. The bite area bulges with pain and fever. The ache is present and turns black and blue from the pressure that is trapped around it. Release must take place for the victim to heal.

In the early days, cowboys would sterilize their knives with their campfires and cut open the bulge to release the poison of the bite. They would then use their mouths to suck out the poison and wrap the wound tightly in order for it to heal. Many congregations lay silent with bulges of pain from the poisonous bites in their lives. This poison robs them of life. The victim is there with no one to suck out the poison so they can heal. Instead, it rests within their veins suffocating any trace of life they may have.

The entries of this book are the release of the congregation. It is the exhale of the burdened, and the first step of healing for many who have been the bitten victim. The release provides healing. The exhales give new life. The cries go beyond the pulpit. Inside of these pages, the pews create a symphony of victory and an encore of triumph! These are the cries of the pews.

This book is fictional yet based on true stories.

Fictional because the names of all the individuals featured have been changed to protect their identity. True because these stories come from a place that is deeper than their hearts...these stories are from their souls.

Sunday Kind of Love

Being a pastor's daughter, you meet just about every minister in town. They are the town's judge and jury, the city's best group of womanizers or the lamest men you could ever meet. I never thought that I would be caught literally, between a rock and a preacher. This is a story I never wanted to tell until now.

It was "Matrons" Sunday at church. This was one of the biggest women's auxiliaries we had at the church. It included women ages 18-45. It was the annual day where we highlighted the ministry. As we marched in, it was obvious the house was packed like Easter Sunday.

Daddy got up from his seat and offered a word of prayer. As everyone bowed their heads, my eyes were locked on the target before me. He was on the right side of the pulpit. Tony was about 5'9 nice build. His chiseled physique made the suit he was wearing look like a glove around his body. His shoulders looked strong. With his arms folded, he stood like a statue carved to perfection. His complexion was a warm brown that matched his smile and his personality. Although, he was a minister, he was different. He was fun, laid back, not too serious. He was always joking and playing with the kids around the church. There was also a serious side to him as well.   When he preached he ignited the entire church and his one-on-one conversation could instantly arouse you because of his intellect. I remember the first time we met, my eyes never left his mouth. I remember staring at his teeth. I'd never seen a man with perfect teeth, except the ones on the soap operas.

This was going to be a long day no matter how I looked at it, back-toback services with a fellowship to connect the two.   I would usually tuck away in a secret spot at the church where I've hid in since I was a child. I would take a much needed nap between all the happenings of a Sunday like this. Growing up in that church, I knew where every mouse-hole, closet and cranny was. We've played hide-and-go-seek for years while we waited for our parents to finish endless meetings. I remember my mother always saying "Girl when you get to driving you gonna be the first one out the church and last one in". She was right. I was worn out with meetings every evening and rehearsals every other week. Scheduling anything on Sundays was completely out of the question as we were in service what all day. I glanced towards the organ and spotted Tony staring at me. I couldn't help but wonder if he's eyeing me or Donna, his wife two rows ahead. I smiled back just in case.

Daddy preaches extra-long when there's a crowd, so, today was no different. My daddy was a traditional Baptist preacher. He would hoop and holler for at least 15 to 20 minutes, each service. There would be people laid out in the middle of the aisles. Daddy said, "If you can't take them to the cross, you can't get them to heaven". I look back, now and understand what he meant. Sometimes the journey would take over an hour though. It was to the point, I could predict every word that he was about to say before he said it. I loved my daddy more than life itself. I was an only child so all the attention went to me. I blame him for spelling my name with a "y" and not an "I". He always laughed and said I was supposed to be a boy but God knows best. Daddy would take young preachers from all over the state and mentor them. Tony was no exception. Daddy groomed him to be a mini version of himself. The fluctuation in his voice when he preached was identical to daddy. His mannerism and temperament were fashioned to match my father as well.

I remember when they first met. Tony was just finishing seminary school. He was in service that Sunday and had asked to come to the study with my father. I remember him introducing himself as Tony Marshall from Tupelo. He was engaged to a girl there, but was finishing up school. "Pleasure to meet you. This is my daughter Terry and my wife Fringella," said daddy. "I won't hold you Sir, but I must say that you remind me so much of my father. He was a pastor in our town, but passed away five years ago. Ever since that day it has been my heart and my passion to take up the mantle and be the next minister in our family" said Tony.

Daddy and Tony grew closer over time. They studied together, played softball together; Tony even helped my daddy in his garden. He was like the son Daddy always wanted, but never had. That spring, Tony graduated and by the summer he was married. Daddy performed his ceremony. Mother and I didn't attend because of the women's conference in Meridian.

I was in a daze until Juanita my best friend nudged me. "Terry, you better watch it;" you know they say forbidden fruit is the sweetest. I couldn't believe I was staring. The whole matron board was made up of single ladies, which was half of the church. All my life, I watched and overheard folks talking about my daddy. They loved the smell of his cologne. They said he smelled like a sweet musk in the winter and a basket of clean linen in the summer. They took every opportunity to hug him to keep the fragrance on their clothes. It's crazy what people will do. I would hear them whisper about how my momma better keep him happy. Half the women in this church would throw their panties at him from the congregation, if they could. My momma was a woman of dignity. She never responded but they all knew from the look in her eyes, they didn't want to meet her wrath...neither did my father.

Finally, it was time for the benediction. Just as fast as folks rushed in the church, they rushed to the back to eat. I yelled at Juanita to get in line, I'd be there in a few. I headed to daddy's study to grab two Coca Colas because they served the generic stuff at the fellowships. It was like a soul food sanctuary. There was Aunt Lucille's fried chicken, mac-and cheese, Momma's collard greens, okra from Deacon Marlow's garden,

17

crackling cornbread, field peas, yams, smoked ham, ox tails, fried corn and Mrs. Mae's sweet potato pie. Although, I hated annual days, I loved eating. Daddy had to stop preaching most times because the smell from the church kitchen had more power than his sermons.

Full and sleepy I decided to go home for a little nap. Momma and Daddy stayed at the church. We didn't live far, only about 3 miles that felt like 30 when you were walking. Finally, at home - peace and quiet, just the hum of the fridge. I took off my white dress and hung it over the door to avoid ironing it again. I kept on my slip and thigh high stockings. Before I could get in the bed good, there was a knock was at the door. "Who is it?" I yelled. "Rev. Marshall," the voice replied. "Tony?" I called back. "Yes," he giggled, "Is your dad home?" "No, they're at the church." "Can I come in for a minute?" I slipped on my robe and opened the door.

I couldn't stop staring at you today. "Staring at me?" I responded. "Yes and at one point, I thought you smiled back." "Nah," I said. He reached over and pulled one of my hanging curls. Everything in me warmed up like an oven. You're just as sweet as these curls he said. I begin to blush. "Is your wife outside waiting?" "No, she's at the church... I came by to bring your dad some notes he had me research. Here they are." As I grab the papers, we both stood frozen. I immediately began to head towards the door. "I'll make sure he gets these." "Thank you," Tony replied. He leaned over for the usual church kiss on the cheek and somehow my face turned to meet his lips. He didn't hesitate to respond.

The robe I had so carefully tied seemed to melt to the floor and the slip I wore followed. Tony held my body in his hands like it was putty. I'd never been touched by a man before. His fingertips felt like silk as they slid across my body. He lifted my body up and down as though I was a feather. What I thought would be awkward and uncomfortable was natural and sweet. His body was more muscular than I ever thought. He couldn't stop kissing me. The eyes that stared at me from the pulpit, hypnotized me on my mother's living room floor. He smelled sweet. I buried my body closer and closer into him. He never stopped looking at me even though my eyes shifted to the back of my head continuously.

When it was over, it felt as though I'd been on another planet. He told me immediately he'd been in love with me since the day he came to the church. I was in total shock. My emotions were all over the place. I was in a daze. Immediately I looked up at the clock on the wall and began to panic.   The second service was about to start.   Tony left, but not before kissing my entire body. His kisses unbelievably grew sweeter and sweeter. I can still taste them till today.   I smiled even as he pulled off and then frantically put on my clothes.

The evening service was a blur. All I could think about was Tony. Donna was now on the same row as me and I felt like a thief on trial. Every Sunday thereafter, Tony made it a point to somehow find me and plant his church kiss on my cheek. It took everything in me to make my face stationary.

As weeks went by, I couldn't count the emotions I felt. I replayed that Sunday afternoon over and over in my head, just as I am doing right now even 20 years later, I still remember every vivid detail. The first man I'd ever kissed and the first man that had ever touched me. Weeks went by and I missed my period. By the second month, I knew something was wrong.

Juanita and I went to the free ladies clinic in the Madison County to make sure noisy people in Jackson had no clue of what was going on. Bad news flew faster than good in Jackson on any given day. The results were positive; I was pregnant with Tony's baby. Everything in me wanted to die. Daddy would be devastated. It was the longest ride home ever. Besides, Juanita asking a million questions, I was playing the whole thing out in my head. Where would I go? What would I do? I didn't have a job. I am only in my second year of college. I have no idea what's about to happen.

That evening, I bit the bullet and told both my parents of my shame. They immediately wanted to know who. Who was the father? How could this happen? Although, to this day, I never told a soul I went from being the preacher's sweet little daughter to being the preacher's whore daughter. Funny, how it only takes one thing to make the crowd go from loving you to hating you. To this day I've never said a word about Tony to anyone. Every time he sees my sweet baby girl, he stares at her.
I, on the other hand, turn away from him to this day.

I lived all these years in shame because of my shame. My reasoning to protect Tony was not to destroy two families and one man of God.

Although, she has his eyes, when I look into hers, I see my old innocence and all I can do is smile. Her curly hair reminds me of myself when I was younger. Sometimes I wonder what would have happened had I just come clean with everyone. Although, I have no regrets, I do have high expectations for my beautiful daughter. My life changed forever that Sunday afternoon. It's a day I will never forget.

Tony and Donna never had any children. It's funny, every year like clockwork, to this very day on Pam's birthday, she gets a card that says "Happy Birthday Princess Pam." I can't help but think it's from Tony. Part of me prays that it is. I see him staring at her.

I've watched him now for years. Despite the time that's past, he's never asked or said a word. Sharing this story has brought a relief to me, I've never had, until now.

-Daddy's little girl

Two Wrongs

I was his wife, the First Lady. Everything seemed to be perfect. We had a great house, three kids, one Jag, a Range and no problems, so I thought.   Being the pastor's wife is a task in itself.   I think the most exhausting part is protecting your husband from preying and not praying women.   Every Sunday, every weekday, you name it and I'm on the job. My husband paid me no attention, as he thought most of the women in the church were harmless. He always said I over exaggerated and misunderstood them. He would soon be proven wrong. For some reason I don't know why he didn't believe me.   Why he couldn't fathom he was being hunted?   Our congregation was made up of 70% women.   Over half of them, were single.   Most of them were beautiful.   They were young. It's one thing, to be in competition with a something that's similar. It's another to be traded for a newer and sleeker model.   Every month, there was new drama.   Somebody was saying something or doing something and it involved my husband. He down-played it as I tried not to overreact. "You'll only fuel the fire honey" is what he always said.

Stacey was my adjutant. She was closer to me than most. She was my go to, my confidant. Each Sunday, she and I would work together, pray together and share. There weren't a lot of people in the city I could confide in. Other pastors' wives were always judging, gauging, and backbiting. The preachers' wife circle was one that you either kill or be killed. It was the rink of terror and mayhem. You wouldn't think so, but it was.

When Stacy and her husband Devin joined our church, Travis and I were ecstatic. They didn't know anyone in the town so that was a plus, they had moved on account of business and they were a solid married couple. I remember when I spoke to Stacey about assisting me. She said God had shared with her that her assignment was to serve under me. Over the years, we created a bond. She was more of a sister, than an assistant.

The Monday I'll never forget, happened the evening of 1986. It was summer and the kids were with my parents in Chicago. Travis and I were home alone for one week. We needed the time together. It had been years since we'd been alone. There was always something, pulling him away from me and the kids. We vowed we'd date that entire week.

We'd rediscover each other and do something new each day. That Sunday night after meeting my parents, we had dinner outside on the deck. We talked for what seemed like days. Laughing and giggling over wine and sandwiches. We talked about all the things we were going to plan for that week. I remember looking at Travis and telling him that I was so glad to be his wife. We layed in each other's arms until morning.

It was our first day alone and I was excited. No kids screaming for breakfast and no doorbell ringing with deacons looking for my husband. For the first time in a long time, I could hear the birds chirping outside my window in the silence. I looked over at Travis as he slept like a baby. I began to thank God for my husband. My day was to start at the spa while Travis worked on the book he felt was inside of him. As he started to wake, we kissed each other, and I headed out the door.

When we first started dating, Travis was a football player in high school. He was the boy that all the girls drooled over and he was mine! I must say, that I am guilty because I walked those halls at Ellenwood High School as if I were a pageant queen. Everyone called us the couple of the decade! We were the most likely to get married and so, we did. We had the largest wedding in our town. There were over 400 people in attendance for the wedding and the reception. It was a fairy tale wedding from start to finish. Out of it came 2 beautiful children: a boy, named Travis Jr. and a gorgeous little girl, named Ebony. I absolutely loved the job of being a wife, a mother and a homemaker although the years were quickly taking their toll. Travis and I needed this break. We needed this time to find ourselves again.

The spa was located downtown, so I knew parking would be a monster. As I arrived, I was informed that my masseuse was sick and had left for the day. There's no substitute for Gwendolyn, so I rescheduled with no hesitation. On my way home, I thought I'd treat my hard working husband to a surprise lunch. I stopped by his favorite sandwich shop and picked up a Rueben on rye with extra slaw and I would be the desert!

As I pulled in the rear drive I noticed a car in the front of the house. The minute I got out the car, my spirit cringed something fierce. I knew something wasn't right. I entered the kitchen I heard a woman's voice coming from my master bedroom. "I'm not giving you up. You have to tell her." Have you ever felt your heart crash inside of your body? That afternoon I felt the breath leave my body. It felt like a pallet of bricks had fallen on my head. I was crushed. Stacey was on my chaise and Travis sat on the bed full of contentment. "What's going on?" I asked. They were both quiet. "What the hell is going on in here?" I screamed. Stacey began to explain how she and Travis were having an affair. For the past two years, my husband, the pastor and my friend and adjutant were sleeping together.

Every emotion flowed through my body. I tried to suppress thoughts of murder. I was hurt. I was angry. I was astonished.   "This isn't happening," I kept screaming. How and why?   "Does Devin know about this" I asked? She replied nonchalantly, "of course he does. He's ready to move on with his life. I can't believe you haven't told her," said Stacey. I wanted to kill her first and him next.

About 3 years earlier, Travis and I had counseled Stacey and

Devin. They were going through a lot. Losing a baby and now finally being pregnant. There was a lot of strife and strain in their marriage. On the outside, they looked great but, on the inside they were falling apart. It's amazing how many times you would pass them both. You never would have thought they were anything less than the perfect couple like Travis and I. We met with them once a month thereafter, just as follow up to their counseling.   Travis and Devin even played ball together every Tuesday. Travis insisted that we help them as much as we could.

"What in the hell is wrong with you people I screamed".   Travis finally spoke asking Stacey to leave.   As I sat there Travis fell to his knees in front of me.   "I didn't want you to find out like this," he said.   "Why is this happening," I said?   "It's just life," he responded.   What about your commitment to God and to me?   I remember him standing up over me. He had the audacity to be angry! The next words from his mouth were the last thing I expected.   "We have to get past this."   I immediately responded, "We will".   Then, he said the unimaginable. "This is not my problem, you are.   I can't leave her; she's far more fragile than you. Besides, she has my child and is pregnant again.   Tiara isn't Devin's daughter, she's mine. Stacey is now pregnant with twins and she can't do this alone.   You are a resilient woman and can bounce back from this". "Not only are you sleeping together, but you've birthed a child together. A child, the same age as our youngest child.   A child she carried alongside me" I screamed.

Every word that negro said in that bedroom ripped me to pieces. The man that I just had dinner with the night before, that I'd known since high school and that I'd been married to for years, just told me that he had birthed a child with another woman; not only another woman, but, my friend and adjutant. The worst part was she was another man's wife and a member of our church. I had counted more than 10 wrongs with this scenario and all he could say was, "GET OVER IT?" Murder seemed more and more like the solution. I began throwing everything in my bedroom at the both of them. I had screamed until my lungs were without air. My world, my life felt like it was ending.

Speechless, I jumped in my car. I called the head of the Deacon board, trustees and our financial officers. They all met with me at the church. Because of their loyalty, Travis was already there. After two hours of truths, the board decided to sit Travis down for two weeks and then reinstate him. Unbelievably, they suggested, we dissolve our marriage and Travis and I go our separate ways. My breath left my body a second time. They asked for my car to be returned after the two week period and for me not to speak of the situation to anyone outside the board. The old me, would've knocked the hell out of each of them. It felt like I was in the twilight zone. Men of God upholding wrong doings! Incredible! I immediately called my parents and told them to keep my kids with them. I didn't want them to be a part of the nightmare I was living. I called my parents to let them know the kids would remain there until I figured it all out.

Two weeks passed and during that time our entire town buzzed with our story. I was shunned by everyone and he was comforted by everyone. He returned to the church and I returned to Chicago. It was like he'd done nothing. It was like Stacey had done nothing. I received not one phone call. No one stood up and said this is wrong and no one complained. More so, no one left the church. My life seemed to be the only one in disarray. How and why is all I could ask?

Two years later, divorced and single, I've moved on with my life. My children have no interaction with their father "The Pastor" at his choice. His excuse is not to complicate things further. Travis and Stacey are now married and have 3 children. They seem to be doing well according to all the email blast I receive from Gospel websites. I see them hosting marriage seminars and panels. It's absolutely unbelievable. Being a Christian woman, it's hard for me not to forgive them... but I can't.

I pray for God to give me strength. Any other woman would've killed them both that day and hurt everyone at that church. I rest in the fact, that God will handle them all. I just don't understand how a room full of people that say, they know and love God, can destroy another person and stand by and watch innocent children be hurt. God help me!

The Bold and the Beautiful

As a church administrator you see just about everything concerning ministry. There are some strange people in this world. There are also some people that have no shame whatsoever. I've worked for Pastor Kevin for 10 years. He's a good man with a lot on his plate. This story is one that has been my secret and his since the day it happened. It is peculiar indeed however one that was a turning point for our church.

Sara was an honor roll student at the local high school with a thing for Pastor Kevin. She had a web so big she was sure to catch him. He didn't stand a chance. Young, beautiful and crafty would best describe her. I watched this child over the years grow up to become a young lady. Her grandmother Earnestine and I were friends. Earnestine had Bridgett, Sara's mother when we were 16. Bridgett had Sara at 15. Their family was the talk of the town. Every Sunday even while pregnant Earnestine was in at church.

I remember when she carried Sara's mother. We were teenagers. We sung in the choir and all the elders said it was a scandal that that girl was pregnant. They wanted to baptize her with fire to cleanse her from all her wrong doings. It wasn't like she was the only one back then. Elmira was on the usher board and was pregnant at the same time. My parents made sure I remained friends with Earnestine because they said it was the Christian thing to do. She didn't have a stable home so she looked to my mother and father for guidance.

Earnestine raised Sara like she was her own since her Bridget was still running the streets and strung out. The only time anyone saw Bridgett was when she wanted something. She floated in and out of town with a new man every time. It was a sad situation, still is to this day.

Pastor Kevin was married to Latasha. She was the perfect girl: a sorority member, debutant and from a well to do family. She was Kevin's match or so folks thought. She had another side. This side was nuts. She was a complete lunatic! While in the day time she was a loving wife, at night behind closed doors she was a something else.

She'd cut herself and threaten to kill herself if he ever left her. Pastor was miserable. He toted his trophy wife around town but the slightest smile or hug he'd give to another woman, even a church member would set her off. He didn't know what her trigger was or how many she had; he just knew he had to tread lightly.

It was summer and we were at the Annual church picnic. It was one of the largest events we had during the year. People came from all over whether they were members or not. Pastor Kevin was making his annual rounds. He liked to shake everyone's hand and give out hugs to thank everyone for coming. Latasha of course, was watching from a distance and observing closely. It wasn't like he didn't know it. Everyone was aware and stayed on guard! I accompanied him just as a precaution.

Sara sat strategically by herself! "Hi pastor! Thanks for this year's picnic" she said. "You're quite welcome Sara. Why are you sitting alone?" "Because I am a loner sir. I get way more done alone. I don't like crowds". My eyes rolled as she finished her sentence. I could see how he was becoming mesmerized by her as she spoke. Sara was young but very smart. "Pastor Kevin, I'm not scared of her".
Pastor looked at me and we both looked at Sara. "I am not scared of Latasha. She's the least of my worries. She should take way better care of you in my opinion".

Our mouths were open as Sara got up from the picnic table. "Trust me I can give you what you deserve. No strings attached" she said. Then she walked away. I could see Pastor playing the entire thing out in his mind. I immediately thought the battle of the year, Sara vs. Latasha and honestly all bets would have to go to Sara. Out of nowhere, like a hurricane, Latasha walked up behind him. "Is everything okay dear? Don't spend too long in one spot" she said. I just smirked at her, Pastor didn't even respond. We simply walked to the next group to greet.

At church that Sunday I couldn't forget what Sara had said and neither could Pastor Kevin. That morning when I went to his office he looked like he was in the same daze as the day before.

"You know Mrs. Ann Sara has me thinking. Not so much of what she said but just her fearlessness". Somehow I could see how she gave him strength. As I was leaving the office to go back to my desk, Sara stood in front of me. "Hi Ms. Ann, I'd like to speak to Pastor for a second." "He's preparing for service Sara, maybe afterwards," I responded. "Let her come Ms. Ann". She walked past me with a skin tight white dress that showcased every curve. Before the door closed I saw Pastor gathering every ounce of composure he could.

The walls in our office were paper thin. I could hear Pastor breathe as long as the choir wasn't singing. All I could think of at the moment, was please God, let Latasha be late. Her arrival to his study was like clockwork every Sunday at 10:30a.m. "Sara can I help you with something," he said... "No I'm here to help you" Sara responded. "Absolutely not," replied Pastor Kevin. "Not like that, I want to be someone you can talk to. Someone you can share your feelings with. Think about that and remember I'm not scared," said Sara. She left the study at 10:28a.m. on the dot.

Just as Pastor prepared to leave his study, he was intercepted by Latasha. "Kevin, I have to talk to you. I've been thinking and we need to think about our next steps" said Latasha. "This isn't the time, Tasha". He brushed past her and headed to the sanctuary. As I grabbed his notes and bible, she grabbed his arm. "It's time for us to move on. We need to think bigger than this little town and these small folks. I want you to think bigger Kevin. I need more" she said like a maniac. I couldn't believe she was doing this before service.

"I am not doing this with you right now, Latasha. I am not having this conversation at all. Ms. Ann, I am ready," pastor commanded with a tone I had never heard before. I went in front of him into the hallway. I remember he looked at me with a smile leaving Latasha standing there. Once in the sanctuary, Latasha took her seat in the front row ensuring that the rest of the church observed her grand entrance.

Pastor walked up to the microphone. His eyes went from Latasha to Sara and then to the audience. As he looked out, you could see the tears roll down his face. You could see the concern for him from every pew in that sanctuary, young and old, women and men.
We all cried with him and no one even knew why. It was apparent that everyone loved him and he loved them. Anytime anything was needed for the church, the love and warmth of the people made it happen.
The only thing negative about the ministry was Latasha. As one of the deacons cleared his throat Pastor Kevin realized he was in a daze. He immediately apologized and began to speak. "I love you all so much and I'm proud to be your pastor. I wouldn't trade you for anything".

The audience cheered and stood to their feet. Latasha was the only person sitting and moved uncomfortably in her seat! Pastor went on to introduce the subject of the message of the day-"Real love". After the service was over, he stood and greeted every single member as they all emptied the church.

I watched from the choir stand, as Pastor took a seat in the last pew at the back of the church. "You know, Mrs. Ann, sitting in this pew reminds me of when I was a little boy growing up in this very church. How I've spent over half of my life here. I could never think of abandoning the very people that helped me to become who I am," said Pastor.

As we headed back to the study, today was the day for Pastor and Latasha to settle a much needed score. As he walked in, she waited on the phone and he announced "let's talk now Latasha." "Absolutely, this is what we will do," she started in. Pastor halted her immediately! "No! I'm staying where God has placed me, I will continue to be a good husband and upright man, but you have got to stop. The choice is yours, you can stay and serve with me or you can leave right now...alone." I stood there in total shock. I could see the weight of the world leave his shoulders. He was finally free! He felt renewed.

Latasha left that afternoon and never came back. We heard she was she was near Birmingham chasing every single or half married pastor across the State. She and Pastor Kevin are now divorced and he has been single and happy for the past 2 years. There's a reward for those who are faithful. God is so good!

Blessed Insurance

Being the executive assistant to the pastor of a mega church is a tall order.   It has its ups and downs. The daily tasks of taking care of the pastor on some days seem endless. My heart goes out to him because of everything he deals with; the church, his family and his personal life, it's a tall order to fill.   When I first met Pastor Silas officially, it was during my interview. I applied for the assistant position from a posting in the local newspaper. The ad never stipulated the location was a church; it only listed the job as an administrative assistant. The description said fast paced and a friendly environment.

I remember arriving at the interview a half hour earlier, because I had no idea where I was going.   Los Angeles is a large city full of nooks and crannies. Once there, I was astonished! The location had a parking lot the size of an amusement park and a steeple that could reach one of NASAs' satellites. Walking inside, I was taken aback by the elegance of the hallways.

There were two front desk personnel who greeted me upon my arrival. I gave my name and waited for my appointment time. A tall figure emerged from around the corner. His suit was brown and complimented his creamy skin. He wore a white shirt with no tie and I could see the custom monogram on his sleeves. His initials were "HS". As his hand extended, I greeted him back looking directly into his eyes. "Nice to meet you," I responded. We made small talk down the corridor to his executive offices. Once there, I was in front of another reception desk. He instructed the secretary to bring a cup of tea. I sat quietly ever so slightly gazing at the receptionist, who seemed more like a robot, than a real human.

I grew up in a small church. Everyone knew everyone and everyone knew all their business, as well. It's funny to me, how you take for granted those surroundings. They actually provide more comfort and stability than being in a larger setting where everything is "protected". It was our family's church where my grand-father was a deacon, my father was a trustee and my mother and I sung in the choir. I knew church politics and I knew the bible. Those two things made me comfortable while I sat there with my tea. Besides, I had been out of work for over a year and I had to land this job or I had to leave Los Angeles.

My interview lasted about 45 min. Surprisingly, Pastor Silas said in the first 10 minutes said that he liked me. He informed me that Tracy, his assistant, was becoming a missionary and would be leaving in a few weeks. I was hired on the spot! We shook hands and Tracy then, received programming to escort me to the human resource Directors office, for all the paperwork and formalities. I was so excited. You could read it all over my face.

The church was a multicultural ministry that was 50 percent Hispanic, 30 percent African American and 20 percent Caucasian. It was the usual church business;   Sunday morning services, few events in between and very substantial offerings.   I had a business degree and knew myself around business models; reconstructing them, you name it. After my first year, we implemented various programs, resources and activities, which all expanded into full-fledged ministries.

That year, the church was blossoming. Thriving describes it a little better. Year after year, it seemed like my job became more demanding, because Pastor Silas' duties became more extensive, due to his popularity and the growth of the church. The congregation had grown about 30 percent in the past two years and now, it was up over 40 percent overall, in the past 5 years. The congregation was largely women as with most churches.

After working there for five years, I'd never seen Pastor Silas with a woman of interest. He was a nice looking man. He was fine and handsome. His golden locks flattered his face even for a man well in his 50's. There was a dimple in his chin that grabbed your attention and made you forget everything he was saying. I had heard stories about how women had stalked him and most of the single ladies in the congregation would join a harem in his honor if it could be allowed. Even through all the attention, he was not moved by antics or craziness. He kept it in the middle of the road. At least I thought.

One evening, while leaving the church, I noticed an envelope that arrived on my desk. The clerk must have left it while I was locking the executive conference room. As I picked the envelope up, chills ran through my body. I ripped it open and photos poured out. I recognized

Pastor Silas of course, but just as Lott's wife had turned into a pillar of salt, so did I that evening.

The photos showed Pastor Silas in some compromising situations. One photo was him having oral sex with another man; the other showed him behind a man while they were both naked. It's crazy how the expression on his face in that photo is branded into my head, still to this day. I went to gather the photos and of course, I heard keys opening our connecting office. I panicked and swept them all to the floor.

"Hey Tammy I'm expecting an overnight package did it come?" I remember choosing my words carefully. I replied, "I haven't signed for anything." "Please call me the moment it does," He said and oh, I know you screen all my mail. This package is personal so please don't open it". Too late, is all I thought. What should I do? How could I fix this? I immediately gathered all the photos, sick and dismayed, I placed them back in the envelope.

The next day pastor arrived frantic! He demanded the package. I went into his office and explained why I'd open it. Embarrassed he dropped his head. I asked, "how, why?" He never looked up. I immediately returned to my office. I had ran all the errands I could, delivered packages to other offices, took a long lunch, whatever you could think of. Later that afternoon after spending the entire day inside his office, he called me in. He mentioned how much he trusted me and expected me to remain silent about my findings and shared he was being blackmailed for the images. My heart sank. I agreed to remain silent and returned to my office.

The next two months were hell. Pastor Silas was a totally different person. He spoke to me different, treated me different, and acted different when we were alone. Publicly, in front of others, he was fine. One afternoon, he buzzed me to come into his office. Once I shut the door, he exploded. He called me everything that you could think of. I was in total shock. I did not say a word. I returned to my desk, packed my personal belongings and left the building. All I could think was, is this God's will for my life? It can't be. Someone please, tell me how you can preach against whoremongers, homosexuality and every infidelity in the world, yet practice some of those very sins.

Nevertheless, hurt and dismayed, I pray for understanding. I thank God for revealing to me, the man I didn't know and his heart. I had no idea who I worked for. That beautiful congregation of people has no idea who their pastor really is.   All they know is one assistant is there today and one is gone tomorrow.

I thank God for the opportunity to serve during the time I did. I believe Pastor Silas knows his secret is safe with me because of my personal integrity.   All I know is, I'm at peace not being there any longer and the compensation they allotted me for leaving was nice, however, my ability to make copies gave me more security for the long haul! I am a smart girl. One thing I learned a long time ago was you have to carry insurance, ALWAYS.

Old Dog, Old Tricks

I am 64 years old. My husband of 48 years is 66. We married young. It was common in those days. My husband, like his father, is a pastor. My father was a pastor, as well. All my life, I've seen the good and the bad of ministry. I've seen people destroyed and people rebuilt. My grandmother, "Mudea" always said, "The Word of God never changes, but the people of God, are like feathers blowing in the wind." I've learned a few things in this life. One, in particular is you can't change folks that don't want to be changed. It's almost impossible...double for a man and triple for a church man.

Our church is very small, maybe 100 people. Children account for 30 of those 100. My husband and I have 2 children. Candace, who is now 43, is married with 2 kids and Coleman is 41, married with 2 kids. The beautiful family it sounds to be is just that on the outside, even after all these years. When you get past the surface, everything is rotten underneath.

It started about 30 years ago as women came in and out of our church. Sure, I know men will be men. All my life, my mother prefaced every conversation about my father with that phrase. I quickly learned the meaning. Even when Carl first started acting up our first year of marriage, I'd call and confide in her. Her resolve was always... "Men are men, baby". I wanted to say, these men are supposed to be different! At least you'd hope.

Even as a young girl, my daddy was a dog, D-O-G. He treated my mother like dirt. Although, she was the First Lady, she was never first. I vowed to never marry a preacher and moreover never to be mistreated like her. Little did I know, I would follow right in her footsteps! Carl was bad, but my daddy was worse. Maybe that's how I developed my tolerance for the foolishness. Carl would come home smelling like a woman and lean into me and the kids. He'd complain that I was nothing like this woman or that one. All this while the kids were eating. Drunken and in rage, some nights he'd take the meal I prepared and throw it on the walls or onto the floor. For the past 47 years, my life has been a complete hell.

I never blinked when he went on a tangent. My daddy could turn a house upside down and inside out. I think me not responding only made the situation worse. I would keep cooking, cleaning, or doing whatever it was I was doing before he stormed in on a war path. It had gotten to a point where it was more aggravating than anything. The more I didn't react, the more he reacted. It had gotten to the point I could cry on cue or respond so he would just shut up and go to sleep.

The last Friday evening in June was set for our annual board meeting at the church. It was actually a finance meeting where we would review the past year and the board would present the budget for next year. I sat in my usual spot, the first row. I sat there in silence since I was never allowed to handle any of our personal or business finances but that night was different. Deacon Hanley started the meeting and announced that we were about $20,000 under in our pastoral account. The money was simply missing. There was no ledger or record of transactions accounting for the amount. There was just one huge withdrawal that December 4th.

Carl was the main signer and I was the co-signer. This account was established when we first took leadership. It was governed by the board to monitor. Deacon Hanley had the floor and he had questions. As a hero throws himself in front of a victim, my husband threw me to the wolves. He blamed me for the misappropriation and the board accepted it. "Why, First Lady?" Deacon Henry asked. My teeth were clinched so tight, one more pulse and they would have shattered in my mouth. I stared back at him and tears flowed down my face. Everything in me wanted to say it wasn't me. Everything in me wanted to say that it must have been Carl's desperate attempt to be a sugar daddy to some of his young tramps. After all, he had already depleted all of our savings. He had withdrawn all our retirement accounts and had refinanced our home all in the name of love. Instead, I sealed my lips sat in silence.

Paralyzed, I sat there as the entire board mumbled in conversation with Carl. I found the strength to walk to the car. I remember feeling alone. On the ride home I was speechless and more so embarrassed. Carl began to rant on how useless I was. Everything in me wanted to jump out the car while it was moving and die. I couldn't hold it any longer. I began to scream. A room full of people who had nothing but respect for me now sees me as a thief and there was nothing I could do about it! Carl pulled the car over and told me to get out. I cried like an infant. "After all these years, have you any regard for me as a person, less more the mother of your children and your wife?" He answered, "None at all". I was completely destroyed. The glow from the taillights, still shine in my eyes to this very day. I remember watching them fade in the distance the further and further he drove away. I was exhausted after walking home for over 45 minutes. I finally made it. I went immediately into our bedroom and began to pack my things. Carl never woke up or moved a muscle. I called my daughter Candace for the 15th time and once again, I left.

I usually pick between Coleman and her to balance my madness. Candace was and still is a much better housekeeper than Emily, my son's wife. I find myself being grandma/maid when I visit. I wasn't quite up for it this trip. I had enough on my mind. Candace and her husband picked me up from the bus station and there I rested, I prayed and I asked God, if it be His will for my life to be in this marriage any longer, to speak to my heart.

I have so many things to clean up. Everything in me wanted to tell the world what kind of man Carl was. Everything in me wanted to clear my name for all the ill things he'd ever done to me.   After a month of no phone calls, no questions or no communication with Carl, I decided to go home.   Despite the pleas of my son-in-law and daughter, I had made up my mind. On the ride home, I told God I'd never leave again unless he took me from this earth. It was a long ride but nonetheless, I had time to think.

Once home, I looked around: no dishes were washed, the daily newspapers were stacked up at the front door, and nothing had changed...not even Carl. He was sitting on the couch with the television on and of course he had a drink in his hand. I remember walking over to him kissing him on his head only for him to shrug. I told my husband I would never step foot in the church again I'd now use the church inside of me to change lives.   He looked at me as he'd done for the past 10 years, with no emotion or regard and began mumbling.

I have no idea why I went back. I can't even explain how I feel. All I know is that something in me won't let me leave him. It won't allow me to walk away forever. I can only turn the other cheek. I guess that's it. This is my remedy, grin and bear it, but you don't have to sit in it. Take a break every now and then, relieve the pressure and get back in the game. I know my mother would be pleased. I'm still a First Lady ...just not at that church. This marriage has emptied me and now, I look only to God to fill me. Like the song says, "I'm happy with Jesus alone. I'm happy with Jesus alone. Though poor and deserted thank God I can say, I'm happy with Jesus alone".

Plain view

"Aww... Mom, I don't like church. I hate going. We sit there for hours listening to people talk and that's BEFORE the preacher even gets up!" cried Kyle. "If you don't shut your mouth, I am going to shut it for you. You do whatever you want whenever you want. In my house, you will go to church. Don't be selfish when it comes to God, son." I replied in my somewhat controlled, yelling sort of voice. As the car became calm, I looked in my rear view mirror at my youngest son. My oldest two had on head phones to mute out the weekly complaints Kyle made on the 30 minute drive to church.

If you didn't know any better you'd swear these were not the children of the pastor. They were typical kids. They fought all the time, argued, you name it. They were ordinary kids and we like them that way!

Kevin and I, pastor one of the most thriving ministries outside of Buffalo. It was a dream of both of ours. We attract lots of college students, young business moguls and just good ole common folks. My husband is progressive in his pastoring, using the latest technology, social media and digital presentations. He's handsome and intelligent. Although he travels a lot, he always makes time for the kids, but me... that's another story.

Finally we arrive at the church.   Gary, the armor bearer, greets us like a secret service agent every Sunday. He always looks like he works at the White House. My kids always taunted and giggled when they saw him.. Gary would mostly smile and shrug it off. Breakfast was always waiting for the kids, no matter how late we were running and like clockwork, Kevin appeared the first 2 minutes after our arrival to be praised by his favorite fan club. The kids acted as if they hadn't seen their father just hours before.

Don't be long-winded today my oldest daughter Kendra demanded her father. She had already planned for her best friends, Tasha and Lauren, to come home with us and later go to the movies. Kevin always had a swift reply, "I'll be sure to let the Holy Ghost know sweetheart." Kendra rolled her eyes as usual.   Kevin of course acted as if he didn't see her. As the servers served breakfast, Kevin looked up from his notes at me and mumbled "You think that's enough cleavage for everyone to see?" I didn't comment. Everything in me wanted to say "Not as much as your whores," but I was in God's house and my children were in arms reach. It was always something. Top too loose, skirt too tight, dress too short, you name it. Never a compliment, always cheap criticism.

Kevin was an awesome preacher, a fantastic father, an eloquent speaker and politically savvy, but one lousy husband. How lousy? Let me count the ways. From the women he slept with all over the city, not including the church, the lying he did to cover it up and the verbal abuse over our 15 years of marriage, to the recent 2 years of physical abuse. I've had gonorrhea twice and he blatantly denied it both times. The straw that broke the camel's back was when he arrived home one night and violently grabbed me out of bed and demanded that I respect his sorry ass. Everything in me wanted to walk out that night...but to what?

I denied my friends for him. I limited my family and prioritized him, even when it came to my own mother. He had alienated me from my entire world. I now had a lifetime membership to him. Threat after threat had finally worked on me. From the custody piece to the "you won't get a dime," I had given up. I was stuck. It's crazy because before I met him, I was independent. It was what drew us together. I had my own business and he was in seminary school when we first met. All my

girls said he was the one to break my heart, but I didn't see it. Not me.
I was a warrior, can't take me down. My "S" would forever rest on my
chest. Three kids and 15 years later, I am stuck.

Church started as usual. During the invitation a man came up to give
his life to Christ. He was 6'2, 210 pounds, bow-legged, nice build and
awesome skin. He wasn't overdressed, jeans, loafers and a nice polo. He
looked like a model. Like a man out of a magazine. He introduced himself
as Stephen. He went on to talk about how he was searching for something
and was led to our ministry. The entire church gave him a hearty handclap.
As he went to his seat my eyes and every other woman in the audience
couldn't help but follow him for a second. Who was this man?

That night at dinner for some reason I kept thinking about Stephen and
if it were an emotional decision or would he be involved at the church.
Sure enough, he showed up that Wednesday at bible study. I
intentionally started a conversation with him and I was completely
mesmerized. As we talked, I saw Kevin staring from across the room. I
asked Stephen if he'd like to have coffee and discuss some of the possible
ministries he could involve himself in. He agreed and we set a date to
meet.

Kevin and I rode home together from bible study. For the first 20 minutes, it was complete silence. The last 10 minutes of the drive was complete drama. He pulled his escalade over to the shoulder of the road. "Kevin, we don't have time for this". The first two licks across my face stung something terrible. The third blow drew blood from my lip. "Don't you ever disrespect me again by talking to another man in my face." I was so immune to the emotions. I didn't shed a tear. I didn't say a word. All I could do was stare out the front windshield. Just then a car pulled up alongside us. It was Deacon Frazier and his wife asking if we were okay. Everything in me wanted to scream but I didn't. Kevin lied out of his teeth and they happily went along their way. We finally made it home. Thank God the kids were sleep.

I wanted to stab him in his sleep. I was worn and weary from the garbage and the drama. Why does he get to do everything and everybody with no conviction or repercussion? Why am I the prisoner? Do I have to spend the next 10 years of my life going through the same stuff over and over? I can't even speak to a male member of the congregation without my husband feeling that I am doing the same thing that he's doing? I can't take it any longer.

58

Kevin went to play golf that Friday morning. As soon as he left, I met Stephen at the Starbucks, not far from his job. I didn't drive so I wouldn't be noticed. I wore my work out clothes and a scarf to hide the marks that were healing. He greeted me with a kind smile and we talked for an hour which seemed like days. Instead of me talking mostly about the ministry, he asked me a million questions about me. I can't even remember the last time someone took interest in me. Not me, the First Lady and not me, the pastor's wife. Just me Sabrina, I felt it happening, I wanted this man to be my emotional savior. I needed him because I had no one else.

"I could talk your head off." I told Stephen, "I am so sorry." "It's okay," he said. I remember him reaching over to my face as he removed my glasses and pulled back my scarf. He stared at me puzzled. "Did he do this to you?" I was speechless. Fifteen years of bottled tears crashed to that table. Two years of abuse exploded that very moment. I began to cry and although I couldn't speak I simply nodded my head. I was more so embarrassed. I didn't know this man, but in one meeting, he felt like he was my only friend in the world.

He began telling me everything I wanted to hear. "I didn't deserve the abuse that I was beautiful inside and out and to find

59

faith and strength you learn to rest in that." I sat there astonished. I sat there speechless. His hand rested on my hand. I didn't want to let it go. "Thank you for meeting with me today. Please take care of yourself." He said. "Thank you," I said and we went our separate ways.

After that meeting, I never saw Stephen again. Maybe, he was too much of a real man to be pastored by a coward. Maybe he was giving me instructions that I should leave, like he did. Maybe he was my wakeup call that I deserve more or that I deserve better. I appreciate him being a gentleman and a Godly man, even when my thoughts of him were not. When we pray "Lead us not into temptation" God truly hears it. I just pray He delivers me from this evil...soon.

Long Road Home

It took 20 minutes to go between my grandmother's house and my aunt Yvette's. If you were walking, it would take almost an hour. My sister and I were petrified of the "Journey" and welcomed a ride anytime. Growing up in Starkville, there are only 2 main things we make happen. We go to church and we farm. My sister and I were raised on a farm with our brother. There were only 3 of us. And I was in the middle. My brother was the oldest and was always on the farm helping my dad in the fields, while momma made us stay inside and either cook or clean. I would always opt to clean because it seem as though it was easier. My sister on the other hand did not.

One Saturday we were on that hour long trek my auntie's house and decided to grab some loose candy from the corner store. The minute we walked in, we heard Mrs. Lucille yell. "Howdy girls. What can I do you for?" "Just some candy Mrs. Lucille." She took our change and handed us a bag. "Here you are ladies." As we reached for the over flowing bag, Mrs.

Lucille had given us way more than what we had budget for. Thank you, we screamed and we were on our way.

Growing up in the south during the early 60's was a tricky time. There were mean white people and there were nice white people. Being a little black girl in the south is a task in itself. I remember momma and her sisters would sit around and talk about how some of the other women, especially the younger ones, would never listen to the advice of their elders. My sister Sara and I would play in ears reach pretending not to digest the conversations, but we always did. We'd be at church pointing out all the characters of the week. "The non-cooking, Mrs. Mable", "The dirty silverware Mrs. Davis" and Lilly Mae Gold, the daughter of Deacon Jones, who they say they caught up on the hill with her blouse undone and Mr. Smith's boy Henry was up there too. Even in church she looks "fast".

About half way through the Journey, Sara had to pee. We stopped at the filling station. I had a bad feeling the moment we walked in. The shop clerk was a greasy white man that we saw around town a lot. "You gals need something?" he asked. "Just need to use the restroom," we replied. While Sara took a potty break the creepy man locked the front shop door and headed to the back of the store. "Hurry up Sara." "One second." she said. I yelled, "NOW!" as the greasy man stood in front of me. "Get in there with her now," he said. I began to scream. The man grabbed my arm and threw me in the restroom with Sara. He looked at us with a rage in his eyes. All I could think of was what our momma told us. We kicked him in his crotch with all our might. He fell to the ground. We ran out the store screaming and directly into the arms of our Uncle Clay, who had stopped there for gas. Out of breath, we told him what had happened. He went inside the store for a good 5 minutes and came out. Once he got in the truck with us, he saw the fear that paralyzed us. He asked if we were ok. We replied, "Yes." He told us to never go back there again and never walk to Aunties house again. We never said a word again.

About a month later, momma announced after church we would head up to auntie's house to pick up some canned preserves. Sara and I were like zombies the entire time in church. We were dreading the benediction. On our way there we stopped at the filling station for gas. She told us to get out, to use the bathroom. "No ma'am, we said, we're ok". "I can hold it," said Sara. Just then the door opens and a woman came out. "Where's Mr. Pope?" Momma asked. "He just vanished," the short chunky lady said. "We haven't seen him in over a month." "Sure do hope he's ok," momma replied. Sara and I just looked at each other. Ten years later, I still see that horrific day. I still see his eyes and I can feel his hand grabbing my arms. The day mare has never stopped.

Family Low Down

"Out of all the people in the world, you slept with my cousin!" TJ just looked at me. I came from a huge family in a small town. Everybody knows everybody and everybody knows everybody's business. This was the latest and the greatest gossip in the town that year. I was married to TJ. He was a good ole country preacher. He could out sing anybody clean across the Mississippi. Even old men told him he had been here before. He laughed it off all the time, but in his heart, he knew they were talking right.

We had gotten married after I gave birth to our daughter, Ebony. That in itself was a scandal. It was a big wedding with all my girl cousins and sisters. My two cousins that grew up alongside us were Patrice and Renee. Renee was six months younger than me and we were joined at the hip. During my wedding, she cried like a baby. I was excited to start my new life with TJ and be around all my family and friends.

TJ was at a Pastor's conference in Kentucky and the church's women's trip, was the same weekend. As TJ prepared to leave, he kissed Ebony and I and told us he would see us at the church when we returned from our trip. TJ was the kind of man that your mother wanted you to marry and your father never worried a moment about you being with. We met in college and I fell in love with him the moment I saw him. Although we made some mistakes along the way, we were young and in love. When I became pregnant with Ebony I left school to start our family. TJ continued on and finished his degree. We chalked it up as a sacrifice for our family.

Over the years, TJ had received several offers to Pastor at churches in Atlanta, New Orleans and even Kansas City. The largest offer came from a church in Little Rock, Arkansas. They wanted TJ to be a full time Pastor and they were willing to let him name his own price. It was a pretty tempting offer; however, TJ didn't want to move too far away from his family. He always said, "If we don't have family, we don't have anything,"

Everyone was on the bus from Orlando headed back to Memphis. I kept hearing the women in the back of the bus chatter and every so often mention TJ or my name. Finally, I got up leaving Ebony sleep in mother's arms. "Ladies, is there a problem?" "As a matter of fact there is sweetie," stated one of the ladies. "Do you know where the good Rev. TJ is right now?" Puzzled, I answered, "He is in Kentucky for a pastor's conference, but you know that." Sister Annie replied, "No, he's in Kentucky with your cousin Renee and that's why she's not here with us." "Shut your mouth, Annie, and get out that girl's head," someone yelled from the front of the bus. I was shaking as I returned to my seat. Bishop Fred got up from his seat and begins to yell at me "Get you together girl. Now is not the time to have a pity party. That girl is your family and men will be men."

"Men will be men?"

The entire ride, all I heard was cackling, laughing and shh... hush, she may hear us. I was at my limit with this trip. All I do is take care of my child, mind my own business and try to live like a Godly woman. Is that not enough? What else should I be doing? My mother looked at me and whispered "We all go through something girl; you just need to hold it together." I was in a daze. I watched Ebony as she was sleeping so peaceful in the middle of all this foolishness. I could not wait for the bus to stop.

When the bus stopped, I was the first one to get off. I looked around in search for my daddy. I knew he was there to pick up momma. I remember my eyes feeling like weights were attached to them. I could hear my daddy talking, but my eyes were shut. All I remember him asking was "Is everything ok, baby?" "No Daddy, things are not ok." I replied. My daddy mentioned that TJ was in the church waiting on us, however, I asked my daddy to ride home with him. My mother just looked at me continuously asking, "Are you alright child?" I never responded. I just stared out the window.

My mother had a way about her. It didn't matter who it was, she was always on their side and not mine. I was never right; I was either over exaggerating the situation or not fully understanding it. Either way, she wasn't on my side. "I am fine momma," I replied. I was so fine, I was about to shatter, weak from every word that penetrated my ears on that bus. My spirit had been crushed and my heart was completely broken. About an hour later, TJ pulled up. He gave me the whole, "I was waiting on you at the church," speech. I came loose like an unraveling string. "Oh really TJ, don't do me any favors, I know about you and Renee, but, of all the people in the world, TJ, my first cousin!" "Yes, but she was blackmailing me," is all he kept saying. "Save it TJ!" There was nothing he could say to make me step off that porch."

My thoughts began to flow 90 miles a minute. I was crushed! Blackmail, of all things, is that the best he could do? Just then, I saw Renee pulling up in my mother's front yard like she was dropping off a package. What did she want? Before she could even shut the door, she began screaming and confessing her love for TJ. Before I knew it, my hand drew back and met her face instantly. She landed on her back and I was on top of her beating the hell out of her.

TJ pulled us a part, but not before I gave her a full service butt whipping. I then grabbed a piece of a 2x4 my daddy had near the mailbox and proceeded to hit TJ multiple times. All I felt was hurt. All I saw was rage, the moment I laid eyes on her in that driveway. My parents sat there, speechless. My daddy grabbed the board out of my hand and fell to the ground hold me. I just looked at him asking..."WHY?"

Our mothers were sisters. They were the only girls. It was ironic that my aunt had 4 girls, my mother had 4 girls. We shared everything all our lives from clothes to food to cars. You name it. If it was ours then it was theirs. There was no line of separation. Family ran deep in these parts.

You never put anything before family. It was what we were taught to live by. How could Renee do this after all we've been through?

I felt my daddy's arms around my shoulders walking me to the porch. He sat me down to tell me the craziest story. He said that my Aunt Lisa Renee's mother was a devil. "Daddy what are you saying?" My daddy continued on to say, that Aunt Lisa had cornered him, a month after he and my mother were married. She told my daddy that her and my mother shared everything. Nothing was off limits, not even him. If he didn't give her what she wanted, she would make sure that she told my mother whatever she needed to know, to leave him. My daddy said, "Baby, I am saying, I know what he's going through." "I don't know about this case in particular, but I've lived through the same scope that boy of yours is trying to live through. I am not making excuses for the man, baby girl, I had to handle mine my way and I am sure, he had to do the same with his. Go home baby and deal with it". Once again, I was in shock.

Just then, my daddy walked clean up to TJ and told him, "If you hurt her again, I will hurt you! That's all I am saying, son. I don't want to hurt you. You hear me now?" TJ just shook his head. I stood there with tears in my eyes. Ebony was all I saw, my eyes were focused on her, yet, my mind wondered, was my cousin the only one? Were there others? Who and how many? I didn't want to know. We drove off leaving Renee in the driveway on the ground.

As time passed by, I couldn't bring myself to hate TJ, but trusting him is what I did not do and would never do again-for good reasons, it seemed. After Renee, (as if she ever ended), there were several more. It felt like a revolving door of women. That Saturday evening felt like the lid from Pandora's Box was removed and left wide open. It felt as though it would never end. To be honest, it hasn't. Even to this day, it continues. The congregation knows and accepts it. My family chooses to ignore it. The community works around it and I simply tolerate it. That bus ride was just my introduction to a side of my world I never knew existed.

Every Sunday I sit in the same seat, next to a box of tissue and a fan. I can't even digest the words that come from the sermon. I don't even look around to see who's there in fear there's "some new". I can't and won't play detective in my mind any longer. Honestly, I am numb to it, now. I am so emotionally constipated. I can't find the strength to leave and I only have the heart to stay. God give me wisdom and courage to get through this!

Some Things Will Never Change

People are crazy! I've been at this church for over Forty years. I was born here. I've seen people come and they go. It was 1993 and I am telling you, it's about time that Eugenia, step down as the president of the Mission board. Why do people stay in positions until they die? It worries my soul, it really does.

I remember our church when it was at its prime. You couldn't find a more vibrant church in Dallas. Now, when you think about it, we were a mega church. Bishop preached a word every Sunday. People would come up the aisles and give their lives to Christ. Our services were Amazing and powerful.

I remember one Sunday, a young lady, Pat, was her name, walked up. It was my Sunday for discipleship. We would take the people in the back for prayer and collect their information. Pat lived on Jackson Street. As I wrote down her information, I remember listening to her shaky voice and processing whether I knew her.

She had moved to Dallas from Oklahoma. She was looking for something, she said, something new and fresh. She wanted her life to change for the better. She was convicted when Bishop said, "If you died right now, where would you spend eternity?" She flew down the aisle. I asked her how she heard about the church. "I was at the laundromat and overheard one of your members inviting people to church on Sunday saying, if you're looking for something, you could find it, here." She said. I hugged her and as we were leaving, she said "I want to do what I can, I want to serve." I was excited! As we walked to the lobby, I shared with Pat, all the great programs and auxiliaries our church offered and how they affected the community. Pat, immediately, wanted to participate in the mission department.

As a member of the mission board, I shared with her the times and the dates of our weekly meetings and told Pat, I look forward to seeing her there. She did something for me. She reignited a fire and a passion for serving and doing God's will that had been flickering inside of me.

Like most folks I have a ton going on with work, family and church. It's one of those things, where if you let it, it will get the best of you. I am involved in so many things, that it's hard for me to stay focused. In all honestly I've lost my passion. It feels like I am just going about the motions for the most part. Some days I feel like a hamster on a wheel. I want to get off, but I can't because I don't know how. Have you ever wanted to just stop and take a break and can't?

That Thursday, during our meeting, I saw Pat. She sat in her seat smiling and greeting people with a nod or a handshake. At the conclusion of the meeting, Pat approached our president, Eugenia. She shared with her some ideas, to innovate some of the upcoming calendar events. Eugenia smirked and told Pat, thank you and we would begin working on them. As time moved on, Pat kept sharing her ideas even aloud in our meeting. Eugenia, along with others, just ignored her comments and would proceed with the meeting. Pat's eyes of passion turned into ones of pain.

How could people be so insensitive? There was definitely room for growth at this church, but change wasn't on the menu. As time passed, I missed Pat's face. In the meeting on last night, Eugenia even commented, "Where is the girl with all the new ideas?" She began to comment with ill remarks and rallied for others to join her.

In disgust, I stood up and said. "We needed her to stay relevant, to grow and now, we are in the same place, doing the same things we were doing twenty years ago." She was a light and now she's gone. As I got up from my seat and departed that meeting, I could feel God smiling at me. My spirit was content. I was glad she had a voice through me. I think of all the people that come looking for something and without knowing it, they are let down by the people that should be ushering them to their destination. I can only pray that Pat finds a church with a people who will listen. I pray she continues to hunger and thirst for the Word. I hope she never loses the light that shines within her.

As for our mission board, ten years later, the same old, same old and Eugenia is still at the helm. You know my grandmother told me once or twice, you can do something for fifty years, but it doesn't mean you're doing it right. In this case, she was right!!

Family Hurt

It had to be 26 degrees outside. Not really cold for New York, but, still cold in the same. I was 7 years old. I loved to play basketball outside. Most times, we used a trash can for the makeshift goal. Oh, how I miss those days.   Everyone had the same clothes, same coat, and the same shoes. The common denominator was, we were all poor, but happy. Every other boy knew me by my nick name, "Skeet," even though, my real name was Tommy. They called me that because there was a gap in my teeth that I would shoot water through. As a matter of fact, laughingly, I still do.

It was 1973, and I will never forget. Our choir was singing that Sunday. The mothers in the church were cheering us on. "Sang children, sang!"   I remember Jessie, my cousin, led the hymn, "Guide Me Oh Thou Great Jehovah:" He laid the entire congregation out. This particular Sunday was just like any annual day, everyone in their finest suits.

The heater wasn't hot enough, but no worries, there were enough people in the church, that we'd all be sweating from singing, shouting or dancing. Boy, we loved big Sundays.

The offering was taken and then the benediction. "Lord, watch between me and thee, while we are absent, one from another...amen...amen...amen! Ma had to stay after church so my sister and younger brother piled up in the car with my uncle and headed home. Uncle Chris was at church every Sunday. He shouted harder than anybody. Ma said it was because everything God had delivered him from. He was a maintenance man and volunteered at the church. He was appointed as a trustee last month, for all the free labor he provided. He wasn't married like my other uncles and aunts. He didn't have any children, but he loved all of us, like his own.

My daddy worked all the time, so he rarely made it to church. He said Ma did enough praying for the whole borough, so he was covered. My daddy sometimes took off on Sundays. He would wait on us after church and we had the best time with him. He worked 10 hour days. He would leave at 6 a.m. and get off at 5p.m. He got an hour for lunch and sometimes, would even use the time to stop by the school, if we had a program or graduation.

He loved Ma's cooking and we knew, if he was home, we were guaranteed to eat well that day! Ma showed out for daddy. She used to always say, "A man deserves to eat well when he's the one that worked hard for everyone to eat". They shared a bond like no other. There weren't a lot of couples in our neighborhood, not even at our church. Most of the folks married were older. My daddy was always hugging her and making sure she felt special, by rubbing her feet.

We made it home that Sunday. We ran upstairs, rushed inside to get out the cold and did the usual routine, take off our Sundays best and put on our every days, to clean up before Ma got there. She would be ready to cook, so the kitchen and the house needed to be tidy. Today, something was different. After Uncle Chris had dropped us off, he came back. I remember him walking into our room with a brown paper bag.

He pushed it up to his face and drank from it and started to yell. "I am sick of folks not respecting me." "Come here girl," he said to Annie. I got something for you. He grabbed my sister and began to tear off her clothes. Annie was 12. She fought back. As she kicked and screamed, my brother Thomas and I jumped all over him. All I could think of, was, Ma hurry and come home.

The more we fought, the worse the licks he gave us, across our faces and on our backs. He never stopped violating our sister while he was hitting us. What went on for 5 to 10 minutes felt like hours. I can still hear Annie scream to this day. I remember my brother and I crying and Annie's voice going horse from screaming at the top of her lungs.

We were all bloodied and drenched from our tears. He commanded Annie to the bathroom, to clean up. I remember him putting her panties in his pockets and leaving out the door. Before he left, he said, if we told, he would kill Ma. Annie ran in the closet and hid. Her voice wailed with hums even louder.

Everyone knew we were Ma's kids. She would dress us in the best on a shoe string budget. She would turn water into wine when it came to all of us. I remember, one Christmas we needed a new heater for the house. Daddy was working from sun up to sun down, just to pay the bills and believe it or not, it just wasn't enough. It was like Ma disappeared. She was never home for some reason. We didn't know it at the time, but she took on a second job cleaning, Mrs. Eloise's house. Mrs. Eloise, was a woman that lived in the biggest house in our neighborhood. She met Ma through Granny. Granny worked for her momma. She told Ma, if she ever needed anything, to let her know. Ma would always mumble I ain't doing nothing for nobody for free. If they give me, it's cause I work for it! She bought that heater, so daddy wouldn't have to work harder than he already had been.

Later that afternoon Ma came in the house singing. We were still in tears and Annie in the corner, rocking. She was rocking back and forth like a metronome on a piano. Thomas and I were still crying and could only watch her. I couldn't hold it any longer. I confessed and told Ma what happened. When she started crying, she made each of us cry even louder. I remember watching her grab Annie and taking her into the bathroom. She made us run her some warm water and we all sat there, as she sat in the tub holding Annie, both of them with their clothes on.

She prayed in that tub the entire time. After she prayed, she hummed and started praying again. Later that night, my daddy came home and wondered why there was no dinner. All she said was, she didn't feel well. Daddy fixed some sandwiches and went to bed. That night, Ma told us not to say a word to him, because he would kill Uncle Chris. Annie didn't go to school that week. We told the teacher, she was sick with the flu.

Ma didn't leave her side, not even for a minute.

That next Sunday, I remember Ma opening the door. It was our neighbor, Tee. "We not going to church Tee, kids don't feel well and I don't want others to get sick." She kept us home with her. Around 1 o'clock, there was a loud knock at our front door. Uncle Chris had showed up. The minute we heard his voice we all hid under the bed.

I remember him yelling and saying "What you gonna do Mabelee? You remember I fixed you, just like I did that girl of yours. Don't make me mad, give me that girl." He yelled for Annie. He wanted her. Annie was shaking all over. Ma grabbed the knife she was using to cut greens and was ready to kill Uncle Chris, it looked like! "I'll kill you right here, you hear me!" she said. Uncle Chris started cussing and left. She latched the door and ran in the room. She held us tight and vowed; he would never hurt any of us, ever again.

That next day, we came from school and Daddy was home which never happened. Daddy was in tears. Ma had her arms wrapped around him. I remember asking her what was wrong. She replied, "Uncle Chris was killed by a car." I could see the relief in hers eyes. Annie looked the same. Ma had told us all our lives that God don't like ugly. A Sunday, we will never forget.

That Monday, Uncle Chris was truly delivered. Even now, decades later, I think about that day. My sister has never been the same. Even now, as an adult, she still deals with mental issues as a result of that Sunday afternoon. My brother and I have issues, as well.

As I tell this story aloud for the first time, I think about all the songs I sing as a choir member at my church. I think of each word and think of my sweet mother and my loving dad. I remember my uncle and the hate that each of us had towards him after that day. It could never match the hurt he left for all of us to be haunted by. I pray that God had mercy on his soul. I also pray someday, we will all have peace.

Return to Sender

"God is grace, God is good, Let us thank him for our food. We fold our hands we bow our heads we thank you God, for our daily bread. Amen." Tiffany always says the grace on the weekends. It's the highlight for the evening. She's grown up so fast. Feels like yesterday she was just wobbling and beginning to walk. Terry and I were told we couldn't have children. Tiffany is our miracle baby, our gift from God. After trying for 10 years, our lives changed, as a result.

Terry and I tried everything to have a child. Terry was so discouraged, but I remained hopeful. Praying to God, I knew it would happen, we just didn't know when. We went through a lot, but managed to survive...even through hardship and pain. Since he was an officer, his schedule fluctuated a ton. It was rare that we had time for each other. We managed to connect at least on the weekends for Tiffany's sake and really our own.

I wanted to go to hair school, right after high school. I worked in a shop as a shampoo girl during my junior and senior year and knew everything there was to know about hair. Terry and I lived close to each other and walked to and from school, every morning and every evening. He was on the football team, so the days they had practice, I walked with the girls. We'd talk about the cars we would buy, once school was over and the money we would have, once he went to the academy. I look back now and think we weren't that far off from reality. We have at least 3 of the 4. Not too shabby.

1994 had to be the worst year of my life or so it felt like. That summer, I had graduated from hair school. I landed a job in downtown Atlanta at a shop on MLK. I must say, that I count myself as one of the best stylist in the city. I was always booked and never off, until Sundays. The shop was packed as usual that Saturday. I was in the middle of flat ironing Sasha's bob I had installed and in walks this ball headed brother with a delivery uniform on. "I am looking for a Pam?" "I am Pam." I answered. "I need your signature." He said. As I signed it, it was as though every stroke of the pen took 5 minutes. I remember him asking if I were married. I causally ignored him and sent him on his way. I thought the nerve of this dude. Although, he looked familiar, his whack game made him sound like

every other hoodlum I passed on my way into the shop.

"Don't forget you're married girl!"... Isabel the shop owner, screamed

and all the ladies giggled. "Hush, y'all know that man probably knows half

the women in this town well." "No, he's new." Mrs. Voncille said. "He just

joined our church. Nice man, no family, just him." Who asked for the

personal ads, on all the local men is all I thought.   I didn't think about it

again, I guess until I was closing during the holidays and there was a late

delivery. The door was locked. There was a loud knock that continued

despite my screams "We're closed". The knocks got louder and louder. I

remembered the face instantly, the delivery driver from a few months ago.

I remembered the dark slender built and proceeded to open the door.

"Come in, what's your name?" "It's Terrance." "Nice to meet you,

Terrance," I am glad I had opened the door, because we were low on

shampoo and needed the boxes for this upcoming week. He loaded the

boxes in from the dolly. "Can I get you to sign?" He said. I didn't reply, but

simply signed and handed the pad back to him.   Just then our eyes met

and they stared, for what felt like hours. "Why does it feel like I know

you?" He then mentioned he went to high school with Terry and me. I hardly recognized him! It was like he had turned into a swan. I couldn't stop staring. Finally, I shook it off and said, "Great seeing you again."

As I walked him to the door, Terrance looked at me and immediately began to kiss me. I pushed back for seconds and then crumbled. Terrance dropped the signing device on the floor and the action began. My shirt was slung in the shampoo bowl, his pants were under it. Terrance was naked within 5 seconds and 15 minutes later, I had betrayed the only man I've ever loved. "Terrance, this was a mistake. I am so sorry, please forgive me." He didn't say a word. He only put on his clothes, after handing me mine, and he departed.

Over the next few weeks I couldn't stop thinking about him. Terrance and I connected on the nights there were "late" deliveries. It was like, I couldn't help myself. Terry was always on duty, so I never saw him. This was like my release. That was my excuse, but honestly, it was getting out of control. I wanted to stop it, but I couldn't. Even as I tell this story, the shame flares up inside of me.

One night, the alarm sounded at the shop. Isabel and I were immediately called, as someone had crashed the entire window of the shop and stole all the chairs, TV's and more. I immediately, turned and saw Terry and his partner walking up to take the report. "Are you ok babe?" he said. "Yes, I got the call to come to the shop." I then, heard Isabel tell Terry and his partner that she installed a surveillance camera, that videoed the shop inside and out. They were installed about 3 months ago she said. My heart immediately sank.

We all went to the back of the shop, to review the surveillance footage. I was paralyzed. As the tape began to play, it highlighted footage caught internally at 8:05p.m, the time of a delivery. As I watched the movie featuring myself and Terrance, tears flooded my face. Terry stood there, with his hand over his mouth. Tears rolled down his face. I was hurt and embarrassed. Demetrius, Terry's partner, tried to stop the tape but Isabel beat him to it. What could I say? What could I do?

Demetrius took the report. I ran out the door straight home.

That night Terry came home, packed his things and moved out. I understood. I really did. There was nothing I could say or do. I know I messed up and I messed up big. It's been 3 months now and he's even hidden himself from Tiffany. That's the part that hurts the most. To know,

that I put a wedge between my baby girl and her father. It makes me feel worse than anything. I am not sure how to move from this point.   I called UPS, to see if Terrance was still delivering, so I could suggest to him, that his route should be changed. Terrance is no longer with the company. They mentioned that he had moved back to Pennsylvania to be closer to his wife and children. I felt even more betrayed. When I look back and calculate everything I really wasn't missing anything. I really didn't need Terrance, I needed more of Terry. Nothing can change what
I did.

Tiffany and I, faithfully go to church, now, every Sunday. I pray every day all day long, asking God for forgiveness and for my husband to have the heart to forgive me. It's now, been 8 months. At least now, we're talking. We start counseling next week. I praise God for all the little blessings.

Since losing one man...I thankfully, have found another. I sit in the same pew every Sunday with my baby girl. I sit there thinking of how to wake up from this nightmare. I've learned so much from being in these pews.

I've learned forgiveness. I've learned patience and trust. I've even learned, comfort. I am excited about the possibility of us working it out. My faith tells me, it's possible. Without it, I would be lost. Even through this tragedy, I am learning.

The Sound of Sunday Sins

Jamal could sing like an angel. He was 17 years old and grew up in the church. His parents were both educated and well off. He was the only child and his passion for music began when he was 3 years old.

The first time he sung, his voice shook, but there was a distinction in it, that promised he would grow to be a strong vocalist. As he grew, Jamal became the go to at church, for music ministry. To be honest, he was the best in the state. He even played for National groups and artists. Bishop was proud of Jamal. He had set the ministry apart, from any other church in the area. People visited for the singing and not so much for the preaching. Bishop didn't mind though. As long as the house was packed, it was alright with him. It made for great offerings!

Over the years, there had been several rumors that plagued our area and our community. Bishop's wife Dionne was a beautiful lady. She was educated and had a reputation of being the best dressed woman in the county. She wore the finest, looked the best and was always on her game; except when it came to Bishop. It seemed as though, they had some type of arrangement. He did his thing and she did hers. Their personal lives were peculiar in deed.

Dionne loved to look good and she liked to drink. It was never unusual to see her at a function, a little tipsy or with something on her breath. It was rumored that Bishop had a passion for young boys, never proven, at least not until now. I worked for the church for 3 years. I had moved to Rome, GA about 4 years prior and was looking for a job. A girlfriend of mine had introduced me to Lady Dionne as soon as I arrived. I liked her from the moment I met her. She told me, how all the folks in town thought she was stupid. She said, "One day, they will wish they respected me." She liked my spark; she said and hired me to be the church's administrator. Although it was on the job training, I took it with a heartbeat!

That Sunday afternoon was one of the biggest days at the church. It was the music department's day and they commanded the service! Bishop barely had to preach. It had to be the best service in the last 10 years! There were people everywhere. There was no place to park and nowhere to sit. After service had ended, Bishop called Jamal back into his office as he did every Sunday to review the service and go over finances.

As the church administrator, I was the first person there on Sundays and the last person to leave. It's was typical. I wasn't married and the front serving counter at Piccadilly could wait on me, if I ran a little behind. After service, I usually went there for dinner. It was a treat to me: dilly plate, chopped beef, extra gravy, mashed potatoes and green beans.

This Sunday would be different though. It was well after 3p.m and everyone was gone from the church. It didn't bother me any, as I got more work done when no one was there. The annual days took a lot out of me and our small staff. I slipped into my office, to start on the mound of work to close out the day.

My office was next to Bishop's. There was a window at the top of the wall that separated the both of us. I could see Bishop's office from the backside of his desk, which was helpful when figuring out, if he had anyone in his office. I could also hear him breathe if the choir wasn't singing. As I was about to shut my door, I heard voices from Bishop's office. I immediately, peeped through the window.

Bishop was looking at Jamal and I heard him say clear as day, "I've never noticed, but you have grown up to be a nice handsome man." As Bishop paid Jamal his Sunday service, he continued saying, "I'd love to give you more." My hand covered my mouth as so I wouldn't scream. Jamal replied "I'd like more, Sir". As the money exchanged hands, Bishop grabbed Jamal's arm and pulled him near. When I couldn't hear the voices any longer, I got in my chair to look over through the window that connected our offices. I saw Bishop grab Jamal by his hips and proceeded to unzip his pants. My eyes were almost out of their sockets.

He then dropped to his knees and pulled out Jamal's penis and placed it in his mouth. As he captured a rhythm with Jamal's buttocks in his hands, Jamal released sounds of excitement and delight. I literally threw up on my mouth. I then, saw the man I had worked with for the past five years, unzip his pants and began to slowly enter Jamal bit by bit. As Jamal fidgeted, Bishop hushed him and calmed him. As he continued, Laura, the church treasurer, walked in the door. She saw Jamal's face on the desk and Bishop behind him. She screamed, immediately. Laura left the door open. Bishop stopped, and fell to the floor in tears. I started gasping for air almost passing out.

I ran in the hallway directly into Laura. She said that Jamal ran out the rear of the building and felt like he had done something treacherous.

I followed, pulled myself together and followed him through the parking lot behind the fellowship hall. He cried in my arms, like a baby. All I could do was rub his head and comfort him. He asked if I could go home with him and be there when he told his parents. When we arrived, I was so disoriented. He and I just sat in the car in silence.

On the way to the house, I called Laura over and over. To no avail, we got out of the car and entered the house. Jamal immediately told his parents. Sam and Jasmine were angry and hurt and couldn't understand. They wanted to confront Bishop at home. As we got back into car, we drove about 3 miles to Bishop's house. Once there, we got out of the car and no sooner than our feet touched the porch, the front door opened. It was Dionne. She answered in her inebriated voice. "Can I help you good people?" "Where is your husband?" Sam asked. I need to see him." As Dionne made her way back into the house, we followed. She poured another drink. She shared that Bishop was on his way home. She advised Sam to move his car to the rear of the house. "That way he can't run away."

The minute Bishop arrived; he was shocked to see all of us in his living room. Sam grabbed Bishop by his neck and begins to choke him. "What did you do to my son? What did you do?" Dionne grabbed her glass and stood. "He's only done to Jamal, what he's been doing for years. I can't keep count of his prey and I haven't tried anymore" she said. Dionne had everyone in shock! Bishop snapped "SHUT UP Dionne and go finish your bottle!" "I'd rather finish my bottle, than someone's son." Just then, Bishop wrestled loose and slapped Dionne across her face. Dionne immediately called the police.

Once they arrived, Bishop began to tell the officers of what happened and blamed it on her drunkenness. Dionne, in return, began to explain how for the past 8 years Bishop has had inappropriate relationships with young men and now, Jamal. "Go ahead Jamal; tell them how this robe wearing fool took advantage of you." Dionne said.

Dionne was released and immediately went back to drinking. "I may be a drunk, but I am not a predator. I got more God in me, than he does in his toe." Everyone looked at Dionne and for the first time, understood why she drank the way she did.

Jamal told the officers about how Bishop had violated him. Although, it was an accusation, the tears compelled the officers to take him in immediately. Bishop was charged with assault and word crossed the entire state, like wild fire. Dionne bailed Bishop out and is with him, to this day. Jamal left the church and his family moved to St. Louis. The congregation, despite their 30 variations of the story, remains faithful to Bishop and stood by his side.

Bishop was never prosecuted and after a 90 day sabbatical, Bishop was welcomed back. He was elevated to be the Jurisdictional Bishop, despite the wrongdoings and conflict. Most folks blamed Jamal for what happened. I resigned my position the Monday after that sinful Sunday. Three years later, I have yet to see or hear from Laura. It's amazing to me how we lower our expectations for the people who are in positions of authority, yet we play judge, jury and executioner when it comes to our brothers and sisters. Why is it? When there is no repercussion to repeat offenders. I pray for Jamal, his family and Laura every day.

Anonymous

"Man to man, me and you," said Thomas as he walked up to almost touch the nose of Greg. "I'm gonna give you something to think about, the next time you think about my wife. Call her again, text her again and see what happens!"

Carmen wasn't the type of girl that flirted at all. She was a quiet, reserved, shy, but beautiful and young. The first time she told me about Greg, I was furious. Not just because he was married to my cousin, but that he would prey on such a sweet woman, like Carmen. Carmen and I went to Lincoln High together. Carmen was a cheerleader. Although, she was popular, she kept to herself most of the time. Her family was a mystery to everyone. You never saw her parents. She rarely talked about any family. Even, at graduation, there was no one there to support her. She walked the stage as an honor student with no cheers, except those of the other cheerleaders and football players.

After graduation, she went to college locally where she met Thomas, who later became her everything. Our wild phase was almost a wrap, when they got engaged. She still had a little wild streak locked inside of her though. She simply kept it quiet but I knew better. Carmen and I did everything together. We shared secrets. We got all our piercings at the same time, tattoos and anything else you can think of. Now, that we're both married, we double date a lot. Our husbands are even close. It's almost picture perfect.

One evening we went to dinner, girl's night out. "He's still at it and won't leave me alone! "Who, Carmen"? That's the thing I don't' know who it is. It's always signed "anonymous". I told her to ignore him, but that didn't help, she said. He was still pursuing her. When I saw the tears rolling down Carmen's face, I knew this was serious. I think you should tell Thomas, sis." She nodded her head in agreement.

That night, Carmen shared the past 9 weeks with Thomas. She told him, how it started as a project at the church, to beautify the grounds. Phone numbers and email addresses were exchanged. The day the project began, was the day the harassment was birthed. That was the only thing she could think of. It was the only place her personal information had been given.

Just like a coward, he started anonymously. He would send messages with insinuations, but would never disclose his name. Carmen thought the person had the wrong number and deleted the messages. Just then, the note became more personal "Hi Carmen"... That's when it was enough. "Who is this"? The shaped sentences were crafted with mystery.

At beginning of our committee meeting Greg walked up to Carmen and I with a smirk on his face. Greg was married to my second cousin Raquel. "The least you could do is respond with some sweet words to match your sweet lips." Carmen stood in shock. I almost came unglued. "Why Greg? Why would you torment her for weeks?" He looked at her and said, "Torment"? "I thought she wanted some attention. I see her every week playing the good girl role. Come on, there has to be something inside of you that wants to come out and walk on the wild side". "You're married to my cousin, you pig". As I argued with him, Carmen immediately left the church. As I ran into the parking lot I saw her peeling out as though she was running from the police. The other committee volunteers and members looked puzzled. Greg shrugged and sat down like nothing was happening.

I arrived at Carmen's shortly after she did. Thomas was there holding Carmen "Can you believe the nerve of that dog"? Carmen explained to Thomas that she never once led Greg on. She didn't know why or how he felt she sent him mixed signals. Thomas in rage, jumped in the car to confront Greg. I rode along to make sure he didn't kill him. Once we arrived, he immediately lunged at him to the point; the other committee members stared at them both, as though they were a main event. I moved up close in case I needed to jump between the two of them. "Don't you ever come near my wife again, you hear me!" Immediately Greg responded calmly and said "I was only giving your wife what you gave mine." His face crumbled! I stood there in shock!

"For the past 3 months you've been pursuing my wife, even meeting up with my wife and now you're at the point of almost sleeping with my wife". As he continued, the finger pointed between the eyes of Thomas, got stiffer and stiffer. "I only wanted to see if your wife was like mine; easily swayed, emotional, and needy but she's not. She's a good woman just like my wife was. You see my man, only few can resist temptation. So do me and yourself a favor and stay away from my wife before I do yours the favor of informing her about you" said Greg. The entire church was silent.

Thomas walked away in shame. As he turned around, he felt compelled to say he was sorry and there's nothing to worry about, anymore. Greg looked at him and said, "Brother, I was where you were before I met my wife, so I know the harvest I am reaping, are from seeds I've sown long before now. I just thought this was my chance ...this time would be different." Because of this conversation, it is. Go home to your wife. I am going home to mine, now" said Greg.   I couldn't believe it. I was speechless.

Thomas looked at me. "I am so sorry sis". I didn't know what to say, I could never break Carmen's heart. I couldn't bring myself to tell her that the man she adored was messing around on her. "Thomas, I can't tell Carmen what just happened. It would break her heart". I rode with him home and talked the whole way.

When Greg got home he took Carmen into his arms and held her. He told her everything. I couldn't believe it. He told her how the affair was emotional and not physical. Why and how Greg was motivated to pursue her. Carmen, immediately in tears, however, she never left Thomas' arms. Todd came by and picked me up. What a day! He and Carmen are now better than ever. Greg and his wife are stronger now as well. That just goes to show you that every story doesn't have a negative ending. There's still hope in real love.

The Revolving Door

"What did my mother do to you, that was so horrific, that would make her not be able to step foot in this church again, Pastor Polk? Really, what could she have done?" Lisa couldn't hold it in any longer. She hated seeing her mother hurt. She wanted to see her happy like she used to be. Of course, he didn't respond. He just dropped his head and walked to his office.

In the 70's and 80's, there were great churches all over the city of Charleston. Prominent black churches were filled each and every Sunday. Church was everything in the South. If you meant nothing in the streets you were something on Sunday mornings. Most women loved Mt. Ephraim and Rev. Polk, because he was a dear man. He could preach his socks off and he was single. I believe the women out numbered the men there 6 to 1.

Pastor Polk was married in the 60s and later divorced. Since that time, he had dated more than half of the women in Charleston and abroad. He was known all over the Country, for his preaching and his heartbreaking skills. He would have you captivated with one sentence. Articulate, masculine, educated and warm was his way. He could talk to a mountain and it would move or a river and it would part. He certainly had a way.

My mother was in her 30's and could remember a time when she was wined and dined by Pastor Polk. She was his key pick. She served as head of the Usher Board, sat on the front row on the Sunday's she didn't serve and was the go-to person at the church. Everyone if Ms. Earnestine couldn't do it, it couldn't be done.

She remembered about ten years prior to Pastor Polk showing interest in her he dated Louise Battles. Mrs. Battles prided herself on teaching young girls a thing or two about being a lady. My mother and others would stare at the way she walked into the church. The hats and dresses she wore from being the "chosen one". Now, Mrs. Battles uses a cane and sits front left with the other mothers of the Ministry. She still has a ton to say, but none of it carries any weight. It's only chalked up as, "old lady squabble".

As time passed, momma's heart grew fond of Pastor Polk. During that time, the church was growing, which meant more choices, new jealously and more people on the revolving door. Just as she had feared, after 10 years, Pastor Polk was finished with her. He was done misusing her emotions and her body. She felt every piece of it, every minute she was there at the church.

Mother crawled in her own shell and closed herself off from the world and even from the church she had been a part of all her life. Many of her friends saw her pain. They saw the hurt in her eyes. They watched her as the world around her crumbled. She only went to service now on Christmas and Easter. Even then she noticed that all the positions under the revolving door of Pastor Polk had now been reassigned. There were new faces on each door. Mother felt emptier than ever.

She was older and now reflecting on all the time and energy, she wasted. Time she knew, she had simply casted into the wind. Her front row seat was now filled with a younger behind, her positions at the ministry had now shifted to others and she was only left to serve on the prayer committee, ironically, the one she needed the most.

Still, as she tells the story of "The Revolving Door" she's now nearly 70 years old. The hurt of her heart still stings. Still in the same ministry, she wonders if anyone has ever seen her tears. Does anyone know what she's been through? Does anyone care about that revolving door? Is she even missed? When you see her, she doesn't look like what she's been through. When you speak to her, she doesn't sound like she's as wounded as she is. When you feel her heart, you know she's missing a few beats.

Now, she watches the revolving door still in action, and sees the young ladies taking the same path she once took; now with a shorter shelf life. Her favorite song reminds her that "Only what you do for Him, will be counted at the end". His door is the only way and it's always open.

Charades

"Lord, watch between me and Thee, while we are absent one from another, Amen."

The benediction, finally; it was a long day at church. I felt like I was in a trance. I was so disappointed in myself. I was surprised, that I even dragged my body to service. I sat there thinking. I sat there cold. Part of me wanted something in the message to speak to me about the situation. Part of me wanted him to tell me what I did was wrong, tell me how to fix it!

I was on assignment for a friend. She had another appointment and needed someone to cover for her. I needed the extra money. I handled the job and had completed it within 5 hours. Being an accountant for the past 12 years has made me somewhat machine. I dream numbers, eat numbers and sleep numbers. It doesn't help that I am single, not dating and consumed by my job.

After the assignment was over, I prepared the report and packed for my flight. Once at the front desk, I checked out and bumped directly into the board chairman Kevin and the owner of the company David. He was a tall handsome man and built. I could see every muscle on his body. As I reached to shake his hand, he grabbed mine and gently kissed it. "Are you leaving?" He asked. "Yes, I am taking an early flight to get home." "Husband waiting?" He replied. "No, I just finished early." "If you don't mind, we'd like you to join us for dinner." The chairman agreed. "We won't take no for an answer." Kevin said. "It's settled then." David replied. So, I agreed.

At dinner, I shared a little about myself, as did everyone at the table. I told them, I was a preacher's kid from a small back woods town. This was my opportunity to do something big and I was taking it! The conversation was great. The meal was extraordinary. Prime rib at $65.00 a plate, melts in your mouth. If nothing else, I am glad I was there for the meal. As we returned to the hotel, I thanked them all for a great meeting. "I hope you can do some work for us in the future." Kevin said. "I agree." said David. I responded, "I hope so too."

It's funny how when you grow up in the home of a pastor, there's a higher expectation set on you, than on most. All my life, I dealt with people critiquing me, about every little detail of my life. It had gotten to the point, where they were forecasting who I should marry, before I even graduated. That's the time I decided, that I had to leave. I needed to create my own identity. I wanted to be known by my name and not by my father's. Don't get me wrong, my parents were the best. They gave me everything I ever wanted. However, this I had to do for me. I went to college down in Nashville. I got my degree in accounting and shook hands with the struggle of landing a job. It was hard work, but, I am not doing that bad.

As I prepared to retire, there was a knock on my door. It was room service with a bottle of wine. "Courtesy of the concierge," he said. "Thank you," I responded. This must be my lucky night! Dinner, wine and now, I get one more night in this great bed. I thought I was in heaven. Before I finished pouring a glass, there was another knock at the door. In shock! "David," I said in surprise! He grabbed my face and began to kiss me. Everything in me, wanted to pull back, but everything in me, pushed forward.

The kiss lasted forever, his body thrust on to mine and my glasses fell to the floor. He made my body scream. He stared into my eyes the entire time. It felt like he was mentally making love to me, while he was physically consuming my entire body.

All I remember was waking up alone, on the white down comforter, feeling full, feeling like I'd been the star in a movie. There was note on the pillow next to me, "See you soon".

I showered, changed and got to the airport, right on time. The entire time on the plane, I sat there, trying to figure out the last 24 hours. The vibrations from the plane put me to sleep as I reminisced of the evening I would never forget. Back home, I reported the visit, carefully omitting my adventure to my friend. She was glad her clients loved me and offered the contract to me. I reluctantly accepted. Over the course of the next six months I saw David about ten times. Over the next six months I slept with David about eight times. He felt so good, but it was so wrong and I knew it.

I was invited to the Christmas party for the firm. I arrived and looked for David. I spotted him immediately, with a woman, who I soon found out to be his wife. I was in total shock. I proceeded to leave, but not before I caught his eye. As valet was retrieving my car, David appeared whispering, "I didn't want you to find out like this." "NO, you didn't want me to find out at all!" I replied. He fed me the cheating husband bull crap. I got in to the car and he did as well. "What do you want from me David?" "I want you," he replied. He kissed me just like he did the first time at the hotel. I lost it, immediately. I drove off for fear of someone seeing and parked up the road in a private driveway.

David got out the car and grabbed me out the car. He lifted up my dress and began kissing my body. I couldn't control myself. He knew exactly what to do, what to touch and how to make me surrender. He took me right there, not even a mile away from his house, where he had just stood with his wife.

Now, that I tell this story, I'm processing and wondering what in the world was wrong with me? It's been 4 years and I've stopped my life for him. He controls my body, my emotions and my heart. Every Sunday, I want to walk to the front of the church and cry out, as I do at night, and ask for forgiveness and healing.

I can't stop thinking, am I too far gone? Am I a lost cause? How do I get out of this mess? The harder I pray, it feels like the worse the situation becomes. Is there any hope for me?   Every song the choir sings, echoes through my body.

Every word the preacher says, condemns me to the point, I want to ball up and die and just when I can't take it anymore, the message rings louder and says YOU are forgiven. YOU can be set free.   My only question is, when?

Love Doesn't Hurt

The hardest job in the world is being a single mother, Steph. I know, I am preaching to the choir, says Carolyn, as she's hanging out clothes. I know, you see all the guys coming in and out my house, girl, I am just looking for Mr. Right. Carolyn was an usher at the church. A single mother with 4 kids -2 boys and 2 girls. She cooked, cleaned and worked like a slave. I remember when I first met her; I immediately looked for the "S" on her chest. She was definitely a Super woman.

It was 1977. Carolyn was 8 years old. Her mother, being the God fearing woman she was, took all the kids to church for 12-14 hours at least. Carolyn was one of 5 siblings. One afternoon after church, she was molested by her uncle. As she relives the story, tears begin streaming down her face. "I can still smell his perfume. He smelled like a cologne factory. His hand covered my mouth and every thought imaginable filled my head. WHY, HOW, STOP. My tears screamed for me so much, I couldn't control them. I began having a seizure. That's the only reason he stopped. As she wipes her face, she shamefully said, he changed my life forever. No one believed me when I told them what happened. No one even believed me! As I listened to her, I could see her heartbreak. Not only did he ruin my life that day, he put a curse on me that I've been trying to outrun and outlive, since that day she said. When Carolyn was 11, her body developed. The more she tried to fight it, she couldn't. By the time she was 14 she was pregnant. Some kind of way she lost the baby, which in her eyes was a blessing in disguise. Still looking for something; be it love or companionship, 2 years later Carolyn was pregnant again. This time; by a one night stand.

She told me how she would sneak to meet boys. With her eyes filled with tear, she explained how she felt like a good girl on the outside, but, I was another person on the inside. By the time Carolyn graduated, she had 2 children, 8 broken relationships and nowhere to go. She turned to her roots, the church. She told me how she started going back to church. It was the only thing that helped. Six months after trying to turn the tables of her life, Carolyn was pregnant with baby three. Along with that baby came the physical abuse.

I remember her voice cracking as she spoke, Jonathan's dad beat me every day she said. He beat me if I were awake, sleep, eating or simply breathing. With 3 kids in tote, Carolyn moved and tried to start life all over again. She dated on and off and in between the men, comes my baby number four; Hannah. She shared with me that each time she had a baby she thought it was a new start. While being discharged from the hospital she met Zach. He was tall, muscular and sweet. She knew he was the one.

After some time, Zach moved in and the happy family soon became unhappy. Zach became a different person. He became abusive, both verbally and physically. The first time I met him he watched me from Carolyn's driveway. There was something that just didn't settle right to me about him. He looked like one of those guys that like to control women. He was cocky. He knew everything. It was, as if she didn't have a voice when he was around. The biggest thing I noticed about him; was he didn't come with anything of his own. No car, no house, no job...no nothing.

After 5 months of him coming and going as he pleased, Carolyn told me, one day they were in Greer's grocery store. A woman motioned me towards her in the meat section. She asked Carolyn how well she knew Zach. At first, she thought it was an ex or a girlfriend and became defensive, immediately. She then told me something that made me stop in the very spot, I stood. The woman told her that Zach was married to her sister and that; he beat her to death, with his hands. He was sentenced to 10 years in prison and after 5, he was early released.

Carolyn said she felt a tap on her shoulder, it was Zach. She immediately snapped out of her daze and began looking around for the woman who was speaking to her. She was nowhere to be found. When they got home, he beat her from the front door to the back door.

My heart broke, as she told me the story across the fence. I wondered where was I? Why didn't I hear anything coming from the house? It was because she had no voice. As Carolyn wiped her swollen face with one of the damp towels hanging from the clothes line, she looked at me and said, "All I ever was searching for was love. I only wanted someone to love me."

While washing dishes that night, I looked out my kitchen window and literally saw the blood fly from her mouth across the room from a blow Zach had given her at the back door.

I thought to myself, why in the world did she let him back in? What was she thinking? In shock, I grabbed my gun and a phone, called 911. There were police everywhere. The officers pulled the kids from the house first, and then, Carolyn. Zach went back to prison that night and Carolyn to the hospital. Later that night, she died. I am not sure, if it were from the pain she suffered that evening or from a broken heart. I know the part of her heart she gave to God but the other part wasn't enough to unlock the endless road of sadness in her life. I am glad she's somewhere smiling, where she can never be hurt again. I just wished she could've experienced heaven at some point on earth.

New Fool

I was determined, to be somebody in Louisville. I was raised with nothing and was determined, that I would not live the rest of my life, that way. It's funny, how quickly you learn to play with the hand you're dealt. My hand was full of wild cards, more than I ever suspected.

It was the summer of 1987 and I had just graduated. College wasn't really an expectation, so while I thought out my next steps, I continued to work at the IGA grocery store in town. It was the local hangout on Fridays, before and after the high school football games. One Friday evening, I had to close. I hated closing because that meant, mopping, cleaning the disgusting bathrooms, you name it. I was finally done. I locked up and headed home. Not even 2 miles from the store, I was rear ended by a black Cadillac.

As I got out, seeing the damage, so did the other driver. I drove a beat up old 69 Mustang. While inspecting the damage, I really didn't see where the bump had added to the problems, the car already had. The man didn't look familiar, but, he was kind and over apologetic. "It's ok," I said. The man reaching into his pocket handed me two crisp $100 bills. I was astonished! My car probably wasn't worth that much. I accepted the money and was on my way.

Once home, I handed the $200 to Emily. Maybe now, we can get the water on and I won't have to keep buying these jugs from the store. I called my mom, Emily, because we didn't have much of a relationship. She was gone all the time. I basically raised myself; as far back as I can remember. She was either drunk or high. She was never at home. She was always gone with one of her men friends. She hadn't worked in the past 15 years. We survived off government assistance and the fact that trailer had been in their family for 30 years. It was ragged and worn, but it was still standing.

Back at work the next day I was checking out customers and the same hand that handed me the $200, handed me $5 for a gallon of milk. As my eyes met the hand, I didn't see on last evening, his blonde hair fell slightly in his eyes. He was neatly dressed and his smile lit the room. I asked, "What is your name?" He replied, Joshua. "Is there anything else I can do for you?" "As a matter of fact, there is... Can I meet you here, after work tonight?" Confused, I agreed.

After work, Josh and I grabbed a slice from a local pizzeria. It was on the outskirts of the town closer to the trailer park and away from the store. We talked for about 30 minutes and the conversation gravitated to Josh's car. Inside, we laughed and shared stories. As were saying goodbye, Josh began kissing my neck. Even though, I wanted him to stop, I didn't say a word. The kisses moved south until they reached the top of my panties. As my eyes moved to the rear of his head, Josh was in complete control of my body and the moment.

Just then, he stopped and apologized. Lori, I am so sorry. "You're so beautiful. Can we see each other again?" "Sure. What about tomorrow?" I asked. He couldn't meet Sunday, but that Monday, we met at a local park. As soon as I stepped out of the car Josh, grabbed me by the hand and pulled me towards him. He slowly kissed me and immediately, my mind started racing. Josh took control, by laying me across the hood of my beat up mustang and for the first time, he made love to me with no reservation. Thanks for an incredible night I said. The first of many said Josh.

Over the next 6 months Josh and I continued our love affair. Although, I didn't know much about him even after all this time, I felt connected and closer to him now, more than ever. Our grab a bite mini date nights had now turned into quick sex escapades. Every time I told Josh I wanted more, he seemed to have an excuse to give me less. I wanted to introduce him to friends and loved ones, he confessed he was shy. I wanted to go to the movies. He was insistent that the movies were too crowded and the seats were filthy. I wanted to know why he couldn't purchase the hotel rooms for our meetings and he simply made it known, that they don't give girls a hard time about checking in, that they do men. For every question, Josh had an answer.

"I am ready for the next level in our relationship, Josh. I am ready to get serious." Josh just stared at me, with no response. I am pregnant. My voice said in a quiver.   If Josh's face was glass, it would have shattered. He crumbled right before my eyes. While I waited for him to rejoice, every inch of hope dissolved with each second.

I have to go. He quickly grabbed his clothes from the hotel room floor and hurried out the door without a word. I'll never forget sitting there in the silence and cold. The next morning, I hurried home. It was chore day and I couldn't disappoint Emily.   Being piss poor, doesn't give you the excuse to be nasty. "Work with what you got," Emily always said. "Go take a shower and get ready for church," cried Emily, the moment I walked in the door. I was confused. The last time we went to church, it was for Ma Lil's funeral. That was Emily's mother. She wasn't much of a grandmother. Emily followed right in her footsteps. We need change and after speaking to a lady that came to the door on yesterday, this is exactly what we need. I was hopeful. I got ready as quick as I could. I put on a flowered dress and pulled my wet hair into a bun. Emily was wrapped in a white cotton dress and had her hair pulled up as well. As I looked at the woman that gave me life, I saw where all the years had etched lines into her face. I couldn't help but wonder, would that be me, with this child? Would I soon be my mother, just as Emily became hers? My thoughts went to Josh. Was he scared, was he ashamed? What was it?

As we pulled into the church parking lot, we were greeted by smiling faces and warm hugs. They took their seat in the rear. The pastor came to the podium. When my eyes meet the figure standing before the congregation, my heart stopped. It was Josh, the Josh that had seduced me. The Josh that I had fallen in love with and the same Josh that I was pregnant by.

We have to leave I don't feel well. "We just got here child," said Emily. "You stay. I have to go". As she began to walk home, I was confused, angry and most of all heartbroken. Everything in me wanted to die. How could he, why would he? I made it home, finally. As I lay across my bed, my eyes filled with tears for the next few hours.

The next day, Josh came through my line saying, "We have to talk." "About what, I replied?" Do you want to pray for me, Pastor Josh? What do you want from me I asked?" He responded, "I'll tell you the truth, but, not here." After work, I met Josh at the Holiday Inn. When he entered the room, he tried to kiss me but, I turned away. He dropped to his knees and laid his head in my lap and started to cry.

"I just need to know one thing Josh, please tell me you're not married. Josh replied with a broken voice. I've been married for 7 years and have 2 children and that's why we must stop. "I am telling her everything. Every single detail about every night you were with me, about our baby, about the life you've had with me Josh, all these months." I yelled. "I can't let you do that!" Josh replied. He grabbed me and pinned me down. As he looked into my eyes, I couldn't help it. Once again, he began kissing her and what started as rage, ended up being another night of intense sex.

This time, Josh stayed the night. I lay in his arms and asked was everything going to be ok? "I'll make it ok," Josh replied.

The next month, Josh had vanished. No sign of him at the store. No responses to text messages, nothing. I looked online for the church's name, so I could find what his last name was. Jacobs, his last name was Jacobs.

As I approached the house, the neighborhood radiated peace and tranquility. The yards were finely manicured. There were tricycles on the sidewalks. Strollers, outdoors and flower beds, beautiful and bright.
At 5587 Claremont stood a blue cottage with a white fence, a nice porch with ceiling fans. There was a woman outside, watering the hanging plants. She was thin with blonde hair and nicely dressed. I was convinced, I would do this. As I approached the fence, she began walking my way. "Can I help you?" "Are you Pastor Josh's wife?" "I am," she replied. "My name is Debra, what's yours?" I am Lori. I've been seeing your Josh, thinking he was my Josh, for a while, and I am pregnant". Debra dropped the watering can. "Come inside dear," as tears begin to form in her face. "You can't keep this child, Debra said, you're only a child yourself." I agreed. Subconsciously, I didn't want to become my mother.

"When was the last time you saw Josh?" She asked. "About a month ago," I said. "Ok, so come with me and we will fix this." Debra drove me to a clinic about 30 miles from their home. On the drive, Debra began to share with me that this wasn't the first scenario of this kind and probably, wouldn't be the last. This had happened in the past 3 cities they lived but I was the first with the nerve to confront her, before she found me. "At least now, he's more discreet," said Debra. I just sat in disbelief.

Once we finished at the clinic, I was sore all over. She stopped and grabbed us both a quick bite to eat. "How do you do it? I asked. How do you tolerate what he does?" She told me that part of her marrying her best friend, was taking care of him, even when he was dead wrong. She confessed she had been making his wrongs right, ever since they met in elementary school. Once we reached my car, I slowly got out. Debra looked me and told me to never go backwards. Keep moving forward. Life doesn't wait around for you, but, it will pass you by. I drove home and slept for what felt like a month.

Months had passed d by and Josh was back at the store. As he approached my lane, I reached up and turned my check out light off and placed a sign on the belt. REGISTER CLOSED. I walked out the store that day and never looked back. Two years later, while watching the news with my fiancé, Pat, and Emily, the breaking story was a local pastor's wife was charged with first degree murder because of what looked like a love triangle. The pastor's wife had caught him in their home with another woman. I began to think about Debra. I guess everyone has their breaking point. I am just glad I woke up when I did.

Finding Jesus...Quick

I need a drink. My mother has been drinking ever since that Negro, Daniel left. I am glad he's gone. He beat her. He treated her like trash. He was a dog. The harder I prayed for my momma, the worse she was. The worse she became. I don't know why she didn't see that he was garbage. Not sure why she picked him over us. All I know is I hope he's somewhere dead.

Momma is 5'2, light skinned and carrot topped. She's super feisty and can make a grown man cry. She managed a local truck stop cafe and had to grow thick skin quick. It's one thing, to know who you are and another, to watch what something turns you in to. As stern as my mother was, she didn't carry defeat well. She showed pain in her face and despair in her bosom. When something tragic would happen, we'd be at church for 3 months straight. When she would shout, all the people around us would giggle or stare. After whatever drama subsided, we would go back to church on Christmas and Easter.

Momma started dating Daniel after they meet at the cafe. Although, he was kind to others and even momma, at first, his alter ego, Danny, would come out, causing nothing but havoc. I remember coming home seeing momma, laid on the floor with her face swollen and her lip cut. It looked like she had taken a back hand from hell, all because Daniel or Danny had been pulled off the road for insubordination. Momma said that Daniel would need to stay with us for a while, so we would need to find something bigger.

As I ran to my room, I thought of every route to run away, hide or just die. Why did she need him? Why did she even want this man? After moving in, the beatings got worse. The drinking increased. I was watching my momma die before my eyes. One night around 6 or so, I was at the table doing homework and momma had just come in from work. She began to cook and Daniel, as rude as he could, yelled across the room, demanding more beer. Momma told him she couldn't handle the chicken and the beer, so he would have to get up and do something. Daniel walked over to her, grabbed her and hit her across her face. I immediately, began jumping on him and hit him, only to be slung across a room almost unconsciously.

Daniel dragged momma out the house pounding on her, until he was tired. Mr. Mosley, across the street, stood on his porch with a shot gun. In my head, I remember the shot, but couldn't tell you how many. I heard momma screaming my name and as she was prying her eyes open, I saw her bloodied face. Sirens blared, 2 to 3 different kinds, creating an emergency symphony. Momma suffered 2 broken ribs, sprained wrist, cuts and bruises. I had a minor concussion and several cuts and bruises. Daniel and Danny were pronounced dead upon arrival to the hospital. Cause: 3 gunshot wounds to the chest. Mr. Mosley was freed on account of self-defense.

Needless to say, we've been in church every Sunday for the past year. Momma cries a lot, but she smiles more than she cries. She thanks God, she says, for another chance to get it right. If only the people that sat around us, knew her story, they would understand why she shouts the way she does. I thank God for protecting her and for providing good neighbors.

Sweet Home

The smell of ham cooking in the morning, biscuits baking and sweet ripe fruit being cut, means only one thing in the south. It's Saturday morning! Aunt Sadie would make sweet cream butter. It would glide over our hot cakes like an ice skater on ice. Daddy wasn't a fan of ham, so momma would cook up that fresh cut bacon and the smell traveled all the way to Aunt Ruth's. She would be at the door in less than 10 minutes before the last piece would hit the plate. Daddy said either she had the nose of a hound or she just knew what time breakfast was. Either way, there was always plenty.

Granny made preserves every summer that lasted through the winter. Oh, how it tasted so good on those cat face biscuits. I loved it! When you're young, you never think of how much moments like this really mean. Although, we were poor, we always had enough.

Saturday was our chore day. Everything got done on Saturday, the ironing, laundry, dusting and the churning. We made sweet cream butter for the entire county. Momma worked for hours on churning. Between picking field peas and taking turns churning, our day was packed!

We spent our Saturday evenings, preparing for Sunday mornings. We would define every pleat in the dresses and momma would make the creases in daddy's pants stand to attention. Our hair was pressed. We'd use tissue to roll our hair, right after, we bathed and daddy would always pray with us before tucking us in. Church was stability in all our lives. I was in church 6 days a week. Granny would take me to each meeting. She would start her day on her knees, praying to God. I would wait for her to finish, by standing on her back legs with my arms wrapped around her. Once finished, she would pick me up, sit me on the bed and make me pray. She wore one ring on her ring finger, simple, but not raised, it was snug and tight. I remember pulling it to try and wear it and it wouldn't turn.

We lived with my grandfather in the house he built. He was a constant in discipline, never fun like my granny. They were married for over 50 years with 13 children and 28 grandchildren. Although she was an angel, he treated her, not so well. I remember one night, he yelled at her for what seemed like hours. She cried and hummed a hymn with me in her arms until I fell asleep. There were 8 people that stayed in that 4 bedroom house. Both my uncles slept in one room, my sister and I slept with my momma in our room, my granny and Aunt Bee slept together and granddaddy had the biggest room of all. Sometimes, we had cousins or folks that needed a place to stay sleep in the front room or on the living room floor. No matter what, there was always someone at our house.

Although, my father was in the military, he would send my sister and me all kinds of presents from wherever he was stationed. My momma worked swing shift: 7to 3, 3 to 11 and 11 to 7. My granddaddy was always there. Never said or did one mean thing to me, but the other kids were a different story. I was definitely his favorite. His wrath could be felt through his eyes. He was a constant disciplinarian for others; problem was there was no accountability for himself.

One day a woman in her twenties knocked on our door. I knew she was a stranger because everyone just opened our screen door and screamed their name before entering. She sat there staring at me and me staring at her. Granny told me not to touch the door. "Granny, I yelled"! She came immediately. "Hello, can I help you?"

I'm here to see Mr. Olen k. Moncrief. "He ain't here. He working, granny replied. Who are you"? "I'm Cheryl, his daughter" the girl replied. Granny almost dropped to the floor. "What did you just say, child"? "I'm his daughter. My brother, who's in the car, would like to meet him"? "How old are you and your brother" Granny asked? "Two years, a part, ma'am, he's 16 and I'm 18". "Do you know when Mr. Moncrief will be back"? "I don't know dear. Just try later". Granny just shut the door without saying another word.

When granddaddy came home, the cat came out the bag before the truck went into park. Granny began to throw everything she had just cleaned inside the ice box, into his face.

Old collard greens, mash potatoes you name it. I sat there in shock. "What is wrong with you" he screamed? "You!! When will you stop the lying the cheating, everything"? Just then, my Uncle Clark and Aunt Bee pulled in and got a taste of what was playing out in the front yard. "Get in that house Abilene. Stop acting like that. You sick"? "I know everything, everything; all about you and her and them. I just wish I'd known sooner. How long? Granny asked, through her tears. How long have you done it? How long have you been doing this and hiding it"?

133

We all stood there waiting for the answer. "I ain't got to explain nothing to any of you" he yelled. As my granddaddy walked in the house his eyes were filled with anger, yet, of shame. There was no hot meal that night. We went in Granny's room and laid and prayed. I remember eating the church's chicken family meal that Aunt Bee had bought for everyone. When momma got off at 11 that night she and granny replayed the whole day in our room.

The next couple weeks, there was coldness in our house. The joy and warmth now, had a chilled sharp feel. Granny prayed harder and longer. She asked God more than ever, to guard her heart.

The next month, we moved into a house because my daddy was finally retiring from the military. My granny planned to move with us. We made trips back and forth to the house moving stuff. Every time I passed my granddaddy, he gazed with despair. I played and loved on him not only to distract him but because I truly loved him.

Two years had passed since Granny had left. I would see granddaddy at church. He would sit in the same seat at church every Sunday. As soon as the benediction was over I'd run from the choir stand just to hug him. I missed him so much. Even our visits had changed. Now, when we stop by the house he never wanted us to leave. The house was cold and lonely, even though he and my uncles were still there.

One evening on our way for a visit to the house we couldn't get down the street for the ambulances and firetrucks. Before I could get out of the car, I saw my granny. What is she doing there? She grabbed my hand and walked me into the living room where I had played all my life.

As I entered, the medic staff was surrounding my granddaddy. I could hear him whispering my name. I look in his eyes and saw the love he always had for me. As my grandma grabs his hand, I saw the love she had for him. All the years of despair left that moment. I saw colors fill those gray walls. I felt warmth inside of that room.

As granny took his hand, she prayed for him and with him. I wrapped my arms around her as I had done since I was a tiny girl. I could feel her trying to hold back the tears. I remember him opening his eyes and tell her "I'm sorry". She looked at him with tears and said "It's ok. It's going to be alright". As he closed his eyes she placed his hand on her face and I watched her tears drops flow down his arm.

That afternoon, is one I will never forget. I lost so much that day, yet, I learned so much. Most of all, I learned forgiveness and I learned that love truly conquers all. As an adult I now look at all the older men in the congregation and wonder their stories, I wonder their secrets. Are they like my dear granddaddy? My heart goes out to every little girl who's ever walked in my shoes. Rest in heaven granddaddy.

He's Marrying Who?

That's all I could say, the minute I heard that my brother, Tydrick, was engaged to the meanest and nastiest woman in town. Delores was her name. She always had a thing for younger men, so I guess my brother fit the role. She was my age, about 15 years older than my brother. I guess, you could say, she's a cougar. I say, she's a plain ole gold-digger.

She was on her third husband, no kids and her lips were looser than her panties. Top it all off, the heifer was big. What men saw in her, I do not know! My brother always picked up the worst women and made the worse choices in mates. His first wife robbed a bank, without a mask or a get a way car. His second wife, cheated on him inside of his car with his best friend. He was devastated. Finally after 3years of loneliness, he finally decided to go fishing. Little did we know he'd come home with a whale that bites!

Delores was a big girl, but could dress. She wore the loudest outfit in the room and had the loudest mouth in the room. My mother said, like children, some women should be seen and not heard. Either way, she was one you couldn't miss. My brother loved her. He had fallen hard this time and it looked like there's no getting up.

Most of us were praying that he'd wake up and leave, but her claws were so far into him, the strings she had attached to his back, made him move to her beat. I remember, when we were in school, Delores would always have a boyfriend. Old folks would say the girl was "loose and fast". She would get caught behind buildings with men. I remember one day, Linda caught her husband flirting with her and she almost beat him upside his head in the grocery store.

The biggest blow out, was one Sunday, in church, it was a packed house that day. There was basically nowhere to sit. Delores struts in the front doors with the tightest dress you ever did see. Her chest was popping out of the top and from the choir stand it looked as if she sat down, the thing would rip in half.   She came up the center aisle and wiggled a seat on the front row between all the deacons. All the mothers of the church and the wives of the deacons were fit to be tied. We held our bulletins in front of our faces to keep from laughing out loud.

It was their wedding day. All I could think of, was Lord, either send a flood or a plague. Just please, stop this wedding. All the bridesmaids wore lime green and aqua. None of our immediate family was part of the ceremony. Thank God, because none of my family would be caught dead in those get-ups. Delores walked in solo. She was draped in white for whatever the reason.

Once she arrived to the altar, Tydrick took her hand and that's when Delores stopped the service. We all sat in shock. "I can't marry you, Ty." She said. We sat in amazement. "I'm not who you think I am. I thought I could do this, but I can't. I'm in love with Sheila. I am a lesbian. I'm sorry." said Delores. We all gasped for air, like we were watching a movie. Nobody moved at all. Finally, Sheila stood up and walked to the altar. Since we're having confession, I love you Delores, but I am in love with Tydrick. I've been with him for some time.

The entire church was in shock. Pastor closed his bible and announced "Why are you people doing this? Why are you wasting my time and everyone else in this church? Each of you should be ashamed of yourselves". In disgust he left the sanctuary and so did most of the audience. I and others stayed for the second act! Delores walked out the side door of the church, but not before slapping the fire from Sheila and Tydrick. That was the last time we ever saw her in town.

Church the following Sunday buzzed with the recap of the wedding from hell. They say confession heals the soul, but that Saturday's main event was too much for even me to handle. After no reception and months later, Ty and Sheila are now engaged. I've already sent my regrets, since I won't be able to attend the wedding. I've had enough excitement for one year!

Altar Call

Cathy said she would pick us up. That's not good, Michelle. Cathy is not a responsible adult. She's only 18. Why can't Tasha's mom pick you both up, if I am dropping you off?

Jasmine had raised Michelle by herself, ever since Tony walked out her life. She and Tony had dated since High School. They couldn't be separated. When Jasmine got pregnant with Michelle, Tony went in 2 other directions; 1, away from them both and 2, to another woman. She was forced to raise Michelle all alone. Every Sunday, they were at church. Every day, Jasmine worked to provide for her.

One day while in church, the pastor extended the invitation. Michelle and Jasmine where sitting in the first bay. They watched as a man walked up and sat down. As Jasmine lifted her eyes, she looked directly at Tony. It had been 17 years, but she knew exactly who it was. She gasped and placed her hand over her mouth... "Who is that momma"? "That's your daddy, Chelle"; "My daddy?" Yes.

After service was over, Tony walked up to Michelle and Jasmine. "This is my little girl"? "NO. I am Michelle". "Ok, I deserve that." said Tony. Michelle, I am sorry sweetie. "You just come back and expect to pop back in our lives? It doesn't work like that, Tony. I am sorry" Jasmine replied.

Later that evening, Jasmine was getting ready for her shift and Michelle was listening to music, 10 decibels above what she should. " I'm leaving". "What!!!" She screamed," I'm leaving, replied Michelle." "Ok, see you". Not even an hour after the doorbell rang. It was the man from the church, Tony aka, the missing parent. "My mom's not home." I know I watched her leave. "Can we talk" Tony asked. "Yeah, out here. We don't allow strangers in our house". " I deserve that" he replied. "Look, me and your mom didn't work out, but I still loved you". Michelle replied "whatever, please leave". "I've changed. Just give me a chance. I want to help you" Tony said as he stepped off the porch.

"I'll be back".

"What happened with you and him"? Chelle asked, even before her mother could take off her coat. "Why Jas, why do you want or need to know"? "Did you shut him out of my life or did he just up and leave"? "He left ok. He left us both. I couldn't say I would have done any better. I was ready to just die, before he left. The shoe was on the other foot. We were about to leave him, all the drugs, parties, the late nights, never keeping down a job... all that can take a toll on anyone. Besides, that ain't no way to raise no baby".

Just then there was knock on the door. "Who is it" Jasmine asked? "Tony," he replied. "I just wanted to talk to you and the girl. I am about to get married and I am moving back here and I wanted to start a relationship with you". "I am not interested in anything you have to give or anything that you want". Tony turned away with a tear rolling down his face. "Are you sure? I've changed Jas, give me a chance". "We've both never been surer of anything in my life" Jasmine replied as she looked at Michelle who had tears rolling down her face.

The next Sunday, Tony showed up in church. He walked up to the front and gave his testimony. He told of how he and Jasmine were young and in love. How they both made mistakes, him more than her. He then, handed the pastor a check for $100,000, for scholarships. "Since, I can't help my own daughter; at least, I can help someone else's".

Pastor graciously accepted the offering and the entire church embraced

Tony. Jasmine and Michelle looked at each other with disappointment.

There a reason the bible teaches forgiveness. Why we are to turn the

other cheek.

Jailbreak

I am now, 86 years old. I am the Senior Deaconess and over the Women's Auxiliary, here at Mt. Moriah. All I can think about is how all these people know Sister Regina, but none of them know my story. It makes me giggle a little, now, that I look back on it.

I married Fred, not because I was in love with him, but, because I had to get out of my momma's house. My daddy ruled with a sword and an iron fist. He said it over and over; I will not raise liars, thieves or whores! I would look at my mother, while he chanted and her eyes would close at every noun. It's amazing how much you learn from what someone isn't saying, while someone is speaking.

Daddy made sure, me, Tina and David, were brought up with the best. We were singled out, of all the other children on our street. Daddy often said it was a matter of work ethic and goals. He wanted the best for us, so he worked hard to get the best. He'd leave early and come home late, always to a clean house and always to a hot meal.

My momma did her just due, but everything she and daddy did, couldn't shield us from the world forever or protect us from ourselves.

I was popular in school and once I graduated, I knew the first thing on my agenda, was to get out of my folk's house. I wanted to travel the world, go abroad, but I could never figure out where the starting gate was. I was stuck, my first year of community college. My daddy had a friend, who had a son and the writing was on the wall. It was a set up. What they didn't know was I played completely into it. Fred and I dated and decided to get married. He was an ok looking guy. He had a good job, he had landed a good girl and my daddy had approved him. We were married that spring and I was ecstatic, I was leaving my daddy's house.

When we got back from our honeymoon, I began packing. Fred came in and grabbed my hand, my folks were behind him. "Regina, we gotta stay here a spell longer, maybe just a year or two." Your daddy said it's ok until we can get our own place." Everything in me shattered, that morning. Every hope and dream, disappeared at the delivery of those words. Little did I know, that was the beginning, my heart would be next.

Fred worked and I was in school. When he came home, he would reek of stinking cologne and cigarettes, although, he didn't smoke. One Saturday, he left; he said to run an errand. I was 5 months pregnant, stuck in the house with my folks and an old black and white 13 inch set. Four hours later, Fred walks in, drunk as a skunk. He plopped on the bed and I jumped up. Where have you been? I yelled loud enough to wake up the whole house.   He told me to shut up girl, before I woke up everybody in the house. Answer me Fred, I yelled.   I was with the fellas. "What fellas? Smelling like cheap perfume. You been with a woman? You got another woman, Fred?"

His eyes left me and looked behind me. I turned to my daddy's face. Then back at Fred. "My daddy don't allow no liars, thieves or whores in his house. You need to leave." Fred jumped up at me and my daddy jumped in front.   "Ain't gonna be none of that son, he said. Now get yourself a shower, some food and talk to your wife." My daddy said. I was done. I was finished.   This man made no difference to my life, as far as I was concerned, and I was through!

That night Fred fell asleep. I got out the house and wandered. I passed every club and night spot there was and finally, the happening place downtown was letting out. There was a blue Chrysler, I watched a man pull around to the front of the building. Everyone in town knew that car. It was Willie Evans, he owned the yellow flame night club. I walked by the front doors and bumped right into Willie, himself.

"What you doing out here, girl, at 2 in the a.m.?" He asked me. "Clearing my head," I said. He looked at me, unlike any other man, not my daddy or Fred. I saw warmth in his eyes and peace in his face. He told me to come on. Get in the car, I'll take you home. I immediately declined his invitation and informed him that I would not be going home. He gave me a smirk and pulled up to the Daily Grille, a diner in the middle of town. The diner was full of white folks. Willie and I sat in a booth, in the rear. We talked for hours. I begged him not to take me back home and he didn't.

I stayed with him for one whole week. He fed me and clothed me. He let my hair down, while I was bathing, one night and brushed it, while I soaked in the tub. Every time he walked in the door, he had something for me. He never asked me for anything he just loved on me. The week turned into a month and I missed nothing, except my momma. That evening, I snuck by the house and left a note pinned to the clothesline. It said I'm ok. I'm doing fine. I'm happy momma and I love you. I felt a sense of relief as Willie and I pulled away. Two months later, I was in labor. I couldn't think about anything, but my folks. I gave birth to a sweet baby girl. I named her Willimenia Grace. Willie held her like she was his. He couldn't stop staring at her. It was the same eyes he starred at me, the first time I met him.

I asked him to get my folks and bring them by. When my daddy walked in the room, he went straight, to, little Willie. Tears rolled down his face and momma hugged me so tight, I couldn't breathe. "When you all coming home, baby," she asked. Daddy looked at Willie. It's not right to take another man's wife. Not right for him to push her into the streets at 2 in the morning, Sir.

I love your girl. I haven't laid a hand on her. I remember daddy looking at Willie and shedding every piece of contentment he had towards him. She's welcome to stay with me, her and the baby. Willie ended, it's up to her.

I looked at my daddy. I told him I was happy. He saw it in my eyes. For the first time, he saw it in my eyes. Willie and I raised Willimenia and her two sisters Faith and Dena. Willie gave us the best life he could, sort of like, my daddy, but instead of an iron fist, he used a tender heart. Fred and I divorced. Later he left my daddy's house and married one his whores. He never looked for me that night I left that house. Maybe, that's why Daddy didn't fight for him to be in my life. Fred was searching for something. I just pray he found it. I often wondered what would have become of my life if I'd sat at that house. Would I have rotted away or would I have made it out? They say, if you dare to dream, you fail to live. Thank God, I am living! Now, when I look at these young girls, I whisper within, live girl live. I see myself in them. Funny, how things work out!

About The Author

Hello! My name is Stephania Andry-Wilkinson. Usually, someone would put their bio here and count all their accolades and degrees. I don't have all that, so instead, I am going use this opportunity to tell you about me.

I am a Southern girl, born in Mobile, Alabama. Ever since I was a little girl, I loved the country. I would beg to stay with my Aunt Nancy or my Aunt Cille. Although we lived in the city, there was so much more to do in the country. Even to this day, I'd trade suburb living, to having a spot in the woods and living off the land. It just seems much easier. I was raised by my grandparents and my parents.   Family means everything to me. I am the birth mother of Kalyn, Kyrsten, Kia, and Kyle. I raised Alexandra, (my niece), like she was my own. I also have a daughter by marriage Aja. My husband is such an incredible man, as he shares me with the world!

Most of my career has been in music, with that in mind, I can't begin to tell you how new this feels to me; WRITING A BOOK. Who would have ever thought? I had to really. These stories are only the beginning.

I pray, that anyone with a story tells it. I am ready to keep going! If you'd

like to share your story, I'd love to listen! Contact me at

stephwithana@gmail.com or P.O. 1151 Powder Springs, GA 30127.

Thanks so much for your support!